# "Is that—"

Walsh's question was cut off by the distinct sound of a revving motorcycle engine screaming behind them.

"What's going on?" Dani asked, twisting in her seat.

"Is that the same guy from earlier?" He glanced into the side mirror, watching as the dark-clad figure drew closer.

Dani studied the rider. "I'm not sure, but it doesn't look good."

Walsh unclipped his holster and withdrew his Glock.

Dani also retrieved her gun and ordered, "Knox, down!" The K-9 immediately dived into the rear kennel.

Blocked by the truck ahead of them on the narrow country road and the motorcycle behind them, they had nowhere to go.

Trapped.

The Kawasaki drew closer, and the driver hoisted an automatic rifle. He slung it across his chest and aimed at the SUV.

Walsh's heart beat rapidly and his gaze flicked to the truck in front of them. There, he spotted another leather-clad figure perched atop the hay bales on the truck, aiming an identical weapon at them.

"Get down!" he hollered.

A barrage of bullets ricocheted from both directions.

Colorado native **Sharee Stover** lives in the Midwest with her real-life-hero husband, youngest child and her obnoxiously lovable German shepherd. A self-proclaimed word nerd, she loves the power of words to transform, ignite and restore. She writes Christian romantic suspense combining heart-racing, nail-biting suspense and the delight of falling in love all in one. Connect with her at www.shareestover.com.

**Books by Sharee Stover**

**Love Inspired Suspense**

*Secret Past*
*Silent Night Suspect*
*Untraceable Evidence*
*Grave Christmas Secrets*
*Cold Case Trail*
*Tracking Concealed Evidence*
*Framing the Marshal*
*Defending the Witness*
*Guarded by the Marshal*

**Mountain Country K-9 Unit**

*Her Duty Bound Defender*

Visit the Author Profile page at LoveInspired.com.

# Guarded by
# the Marshal

## SHAREE STOVER

**LOVE INSPIRED** SUSPENSE
INSPIRATIONAL ROMANCE

**LOVE INSPIRED® SUSPENSE**
INSPIRATIONAL ROMANCE

ISBN-13: 978-1-335-63828-1

Guarded by the Marshal

Copyright © 2024 by Sharee Stover

Recycling programs for this product may not exist in your area.

Love Inspired
22 Adelaide St. West, 41st Floor
Toronto, Ontario M5H 4E3, Canada
www.LoveInspired.com

**Printed in Lithuania**

MIX
Paper | Supporting responsible forestry
FSC® C021394

And ye are complete in him,
which is the head of all principality and power.
—*Colossians* 2:10

This book is dedicated to those enduring a
season of change and transition.
With God, you're never alone!

# ONE

"I'm confused how evidence in an ongoing investigation disappears." Heartland Fugitive Task Force commander Beckham Walsh restrained his irritation while staring at the woman he'd avoided for nearly three decades. "What process did your department neglect?"

Grand Island police chief Danielle Fontaine squared her shoulders from behind her desk. Long, chestnut layers framed her oval face. Her defensive posture, complete with narrowed brown eyes, shadowed by thick lashes, and pursed full lips, reminded Walsh of her as a young recruit. Stubborn, determined, and gorgeous. All the traits that had attracted him in the beginning of their relationship three decades prior still applied.

"I assure you, we will figure out what's going on."

"Dani," Walsh said, using her nickname, "that's a placating comment."

She sighed. "I wasn't in command when your team secured the evidence here. I'm unaware of the particulars of this specific case. Please bring me up to speed."

"The munitions are part of a multi-jurisdictional illegal weapons operation. Enrique Prachank, the trafficking leader, is a fugitive and about as slippery as an oiled catfish. He's eluded capture for over a year."

Dani sucked in a breath. "Your case is connected to Prachank?"

"Yeah." Walsh paused. "You're aware of him?"

"Isn't everyone in law enforcement?" Worry replaced the calm she'd exuded. "I'm not defending or minimizing the situation, but only one of those guns is unaccounted for." Still, that missing firearm was tied to Prachank's many crimes, including arms and drugs dealing. The evidence could help bring Prachank down. Now they needed to determine how it'd disappeared from the Grand Island PD.

"It reflects a compromise in the chain of custody, jeopardizing the entire case," Walsh concluded, conveying the seriousness of the implication.

Glancing at his watch, he winced: 2030. The late hour wasn't helping his attitude at all. Thirty years of combined experience between the military and law enforcement, and the never-ending war on incompetence persisted. Still, grace overrode accusations and his goal was resolution, not blame.

"I'm certain at worst it's a labeling issue," Dani said.

"If you believed that, you wouldn't have called me here," Walsh contended.

"I didn't." She lifted her chin, challenging him. "As a courtesy, I notified you of the anonymous text advising the case number and missing item."

Recollections of the intense takedown that HFTF had diligently pursued bounced to the forefront of his mind. Months of hard work, sacrifices, and stress to keep the cache of illegal weapons off the streets was now threatened.

"I'll get to the bottom of it when I speak with Jayne Bardot, my evidence technician."

"Why haven't you done that already?" The words came out harsher than he'd intended.

Dani quirked an aggravated brow. "She's unavailable. Jayne's a trusted employee, and I have confidence she'll clear this matter to your satisfaction."

Walsh huffed out a breath. It was like they'd traveled back in time and replayed their original roles.

Him the accuser, Dani the defender.

The repeat of their past, resulting in the subsequent rupture of their relationship, wasn't an event he wanted to revisit. Yet, here they were, circling the same mountain nearly thirty years later.

"Send the security footage to my team." He gestured at her computer monitor. "We'll scan for intruders." And anything else that revealed the truth.

"I've reviewed the videos and found nothing suspicious," Dani argued.

"Great." Walsh forced a smile. "Then it won't hurt for us to do it again." *The right way.*

They held their silent standoff.

Only the sleek black dog splayed at her feet moved, stretching his legs and squeaking out a yawn. Walsh glanced down, a grin tugging at his lips, and addressed Dani, "May I pet him?"

"Sure, his name is Knox."

The moment lightened the tension as Walsh knelt to stroke the dog's short coal-colored fur.

"He's a purebred mutt."

"Those are the best, right?" Walsh spoke to Knox. "He has a lot of Doberman features."

The dog shifted into a regal sphinx position, offering a better view of his narrow brown-and-black snout.

"He's got Great Dane blood mixed in, too." She offered him a dog biscuit from a box in her desk.

Walsh passed it to Knox, who happily munched on the treat.

Dani's disposition softened with the canine deflection. Walsh shifted into investigator mode, aiming to gain her trust with the common interest. "What're his specialties?"

"Evidence recovery and explosives detection."

*Ironic, considering Dani's department lost the evidence which was their current topic of discussion.* The thought lingered on his lips. He withheld it thanks to the throw-no-stones reminder nudging his conscience. He considered his failures, which left his heart and ego forever scarred. Walsh's career centered around protecting others, and he'd botched that job with the most important person in his life. A flash of his deceased wife, Gwen, flitted to mind unbidden. Walsh shoved it away. That was a long time ago. He couldn't change her outcome, nor did he fear a recurrence. Living as a bachelor ensured he'd never face that pain again. A ring erupted from Dani's pocket, jolting Walsh to the present. He perched on her desk, leaning closer to eavesdrop.

Dani frowned, pushing back in her chair to create distance. "It's Jayne. I'll answer on speakerphone."

Walsh nodded but didn't move. Speaking to the evidence tech was of utmost importance.

She swiped the screen. "Hey, I've been—"

"I must talk to you. Now. It's urgent!" the woman screeched into the line. "Not on the phone, only in person."

"Jayne, what's wrong?" Compassion overrode Dani's question.

"Please hurry!"

"Okay. Where are you?" She spoke calmly, though Walsh didn't miss the concern in her expression.

"Meet me at the abandoned Mills Warehouse off County Road 436 in Broken Bow."

"Jayne?" Dani glanced at the device, as if expecting it to explain. "She hung up. Did you get all that?"

"Yes, let's go." He jumped to his feet.

"It's unnecessary for you to accompany me."

"Negative." Walsh set his jaw. "Nonnegotiable."

"Fine." Dani dragged the word for several syllables. "You drive," she said, resuming control of the situation.

Walsh grinned at the ploy.

Knox barked, quickly standing on all fours.

"Sorry, you wait here until I return," Dani said.

"He's welcome to join us." If he wasn't mistaken, Dani's hardened expression softened.

She holstered her duty weapon and snagged a leash from the hook by the door. "In that case, come on, Knox."

The Dobie mix trotted to her side.

Walsh led the way to his black SUV and settled Knox in the kennel behind the front seats. "We equip our SUVs with canine kennels and supplies." The sudden realization that he'd said that to impress her had his neck warming.

"Wow, that's very cool." Dani was seat-belted and waiting when he slid behind the wheel. Her purse rested as a barrier between them. "Knox and I are always together since Lincoln PD partnered us eight years ago."

That captured Walsh's interest. "I wasn't aware you were a handler." He didn't know anything about the woman he'd avoided at all costs after their clash.

"I retired Knox when I took the GIPD promotion. He's still adjusting."

With the impact of a swift kick to the gut, Walsh struggled not to react to her words, contemplating his own impending mandatory retirement. A poisonous snake threatening to strike and take him out of the game.

Shoving aside the dread, he reverted to his best defense—avoidance and denial. "Dogs are an intricate part of HFTF. We owe them several team successes."

"HFTF's reputation is unsurpassed." Dani surprised him with the compliment, and the short reprieve from their heated discussion lessened Walsh's tension. "Thanks. I didn't realize you'd taken the job at GIPD."

She nodded. "Recently, and I'm sorry for this mess. There is no excuse for the evidence issue. You have my word that I will rectify and ensure this doesn't happen again."

"How well do you know Jayne?"

"She's a sweet young woman and a responsible single mother."

Walsh noticed Dani's stiffened posture. Fabulous. He'd put her back on the defensive. "Does she normally call panicked and demanding your attention like this on a Friday night?"

Dani hesitated, conveying more than her words. "No," she replied. "She's high-strung. Most likely, whatever is happening isn't as bad as she made it sound."

"Trying to convince me or you?"

"Both, I guess." She shrugged and looked out her window. "We met at a women's ministry lunch about a year ago. We've become close friends. She's a great asset to the department."

"Aha, you went into rescue mode," Walsh surmised, then clamped his mouth shut, fearing he'd offended Dani again.

"Probably." Her gentle response relieved him. "Most cops possess the rescuer mentality. It's why we pursue law enforcement careers."

"No shame in that," he added, hoping to maintain the cordial conversation.

Dani quieted, and he traversed his thoughts. Why, after three decades, had their paths intersected? Should he broach the topic, or would that erect bitter walls?

They drove for a half hour in silence before Walsh

said, "I'm not familiar with Broken Bow, so you'll have to guide me."

"Broken Bow is a town northwest of Grand Island, boasting a population of a little over three thousand."

"Impressive."

The corner of Dani's lip quirked. "That's one of the few benefits of growing up in this area." She provided directions through the country landscape.

At last, the warehouse loomed ahead.

"Take the frontage road instead." She gestured to a lane that paralleled the building.

"Perimeter check," Walsh deduced.

"Right."

"There are binoculars in the console."

Dani withdrew them, surveying their surroundings.

Walsh turned off the headlights and carefully navigated the dirt grooves. Thanks to Nebraska's summer drought, the road mimicked desert conditions. It also eliminated proof of whether the tracks were recent. They drove around the perimeter, then moved toward the building.

"Clear." Dani replaced the binoculars. "That's Jayne's maroon sedan under that oak tree."

He parked beside the vehicle and shut off the engine. Dani exited the SUV, then released Knox, snapping on his leash. Walsh checked his magazine and with his gun in hand, the trio approached the warehouse.

He gripped the door handle and tugged. "It's locked."

"Maybe she went through the side entrance."

They reached the east entrance and stepped in, allowing the door to close softly. A glow at the far corner provided the only light in the expanse.

"Jayne?" Dani's voice echoed in the eerie darkness.

Walsh touched her arm, lifting his Glock slightly in reminder. He'd activated his weapon-mounted flashlight and swept the beam around the room. Dani looped Knox's leash over her wrist and withdrew her gun, mimicking Walsh's moves. They proceeded cautiously.

Boxes wrapped in plastic and set on pallets consumed the area.

Decaying grain and something pungent assailed his senses. Their boots padded on the cement floor as they surveilled the warehouse. A figure emerged, looming in the shadows in an alcove between two large stacks of pallets.

"Dani!" A willowy woman burst forward, arms outstretched. "Thank you for coming!" Her long, dark hair fluttered like a cape as she rushed toward them.

Dani holstered her weapon. "What's going—"

"I don't think he followed me." Jayne's wide blue eyes bounced around the room, landing on Walsh for a second before scanning the warehouse.

"Who?" Walsh kept his gun at the ready, surveying the dim space.

Jayne shook her head. "It's important you find—"

Rapid shots cut off her sentence.

Instinctively, Walsh and Dani tackled Jayne and Knox to the floor in a synchronized effort. She and

Walsh pushed them into the safety of the corridor and returned fire.

The hollow room amplified the deafening sounds as though a hundred guns shot back.

"Dani." Jayne's voice was soft behind them.

She lifted a hand, silencing her friend without turning to address her. They needed to focus on the return assault.

Then, as quickly as it began, the gunfire ceased.

Dani and Walsh held their positions, not daring to move.

A thud preceded an explosion. A flash-bang grenade erupted, blinding and deafening them.

Walsh ducked, blinking hard. "Stay here." He shifted ahead of Dani, eyes stinging, and bolted after the shooter.

Dani maintained cover for Walsh through her blurred vision, then turned to check on Jayne.

Eyes closed, her friend's head lolled to the side.

"No, no." Dani scurried closer, brushing her knee against Jayne's outstretched arm.

A brass key rested in her open palm.

Dani's attention shifted to the spreading crimson stain seeping through Jayne's pale-yellow T-shirt. "Walsh!"

When he didn't immediately respond, Dani hollered louder. "Walsh!"

A slamming door and heavy footfalls drew closer. "Dani!"

"I'm here! Call 9-1-1!" Her gun, weapon light still activated, lay on the ground.

He skidded to a halt, his six-foot-four-inch frame towering in front of her. "Were you hit?" He withdrew his cell phone and dialed on speakerphone.

"No. Jayne's hurt." Dani held her in an awkward embrace. "I can't see where."

"Is she—"

"No." Dani pressed her fingers to Jayne's neck. "She's got a faint pulse."

The line rang twice before a woman answered. "Nine-one-one, what's your—"

"This is deputy US marshal, Commander Walsh," he barked. "I need an ambulance at the abandoned Mills Warehouse. Patient is female, mid-thirties, GSW to the chest. Pulse is slight and erratic."

"EMTs are en route," the operator responded.

Walsh disconnected. "Let's get her into the recovery position."

She nodded.

They positioned Jayne on her right side, her top leg bent to brace her knee on the ground, then straightened her right leg. Walsh adjusted Jayne's arms, sliding one straight above her head and tucking the other under her cheek.

He dug into his pockets, then tugged off his T-shirt, exposing the black compression shirt underneath. "Use this to absorb the blood."

Dani held the tan fabric against the wound, soaking it within seconds. They had to get Jayne to the hospital before she bled to death.

Knox paced, whining softly.

"Did you check him over for injuries, too?"

She blinked, processing Walsh's question.

"Dani?" He placed a beefy hand on her shoulder. Like an electric shock, his touch jolted her to the present.

"Come here, Knox," she cooed, snapping out of her daze and shrugging off Walsh. She detested the quiver in her voice as she groped the dog's short fur. "He's okay."

"Good."

"I was certain I'd moved fast enough to protect her." She stroked Jayne's dark hair away from her face. "I'm so sorry. Lord, we need You. Please help her," she prayed aloud.

"Help's on the way," Walsh assured her.

"I don't understand what happened here."

Knox sat beside her and nudged her arm with his cold nose.

"I'm glad you're okay," she whispered before returning her focus to Jayne. "How? Why?"

"I'll secure the scene while you ride in the rig with her." Walsh's steady response reminded Dani of her responsibilities.

She was a cop first, and she'd not fall apart.

Especially not in front of Walsh.

"No. I'm needed here." Dani stood, shoulders back. "Were you able to trace the shooter's escape? See what he drove?" She assumed her command composure, emotionally distancing herself from the situation.

"I walked the perimeter and saw no tracks, though it's hard to tell with the hardened earth." Walsh gripped his cell phone. "Pretty sure he exited through the south door."

Dani shook her head. "There were no other cars besides Jayne's."

"He could've driven a UTV and hidden it in the tree line." He hesitated. "Unless he was waiting to ambush us." Suspicion hovered in his tone.

"What're you saying?"

"Jayne lured you here."

"She did not!"

Walsh frowned but didn't respond.

"Maybe he broke the window to escape after tossing the flash-bang?"

"Negative, the glass is on the inside."

Dani glanced at Jayne. The implications slammed into her with the force of a hurricane.

She'd failed to protect her friend. Jayne worked hard, balancing her role as a single mother with her job at the PD. An impossible task in divided devotions in Dani's opinion. She should know—her mother's daily struggle to be enough was proof.

Dani had surrendered everything for her career, believing her ex-husband Mark's promises that their marriage was all he'd needed. Instead, he'd abandoned her for a younger woman with whom he'd built a beautiful family. The same obligations he'd sworn he hadn't wanted from Dani. Just as her father had done to her mother, trading them in for something better.

Bitterness welled within her at history's cruel propensity to repeat. Never again would she succumb to that pain.

Dani swallowed the emotions rising like bile in her throat.

Why hadn't she protected Jayne? She'd take her place this instant! Dani's sole existence, other than her job, affected no one else. "She tried to warn me," Dani whispered.

Dani was expendable. Jayne was young and had so much life to live. She had an infant daughter who relied on her, especially after Tessa's drug-addict father had overdosed. Tessa would be an orphan if Jayne died.

"Tessa!" Dani blurted.

Walsh faced her.

"We have to check on Jayne's baby as soon as we get out of here." The six-month-old had no one else. No wonder Jayne had made Dani promise to care for Tessa if anything happened to her. Had Jayne feared she was in danger? Where was Tessa now?

"Okay. Rescue is coming. We'll take care of Tessa once Jayne is transported." Walsh pocketed his phone. "Locals will process the crime scene."

"No!" She whipped her head to look at him. "I'm handling the investigation."

"Dani." Walsh's annoyingly calm composure teetered on placating. "We need objectivity."

He was right, and she hated admitting that. They were outside her jurisdiction. She studied her ex-boyfriend, and the idea bloomed.

"Fine. Then let your team do it." Dani checked Jayne's wound again. HFTF's success rate was unsurpassed among neighboring task forces. Walsh couldn't argue that. She knew of the interagency task force's cooperative efforts with the FBI, ATF, US Marshals, and other local agencies in Nebraska, Iowa, and South Dakota. They'd sort this out.

"She deserves the best. Please." She'd never spoken more honest words. Loath to admit her desperation, her concern for Jayne overrode her intentional standoffishness with Beckham Walsh. Regardless of their past, Jayne needed their help.

He sighed. Not infuriation, rather resignation. "Okay."

"I'd like to be included in the case."

He seemed to study her before dialing and selecting speakerphone. Dani appreciated his willingness to let her participate in the discussion.

"Heartland Fugitive Task Force," a woman answered.

"Eliana, please initiate a team conference call," Walsh said.

"I'll patch them in," she responded. Within a few seconds, several clicks confirmed the joining members.

"Grand Island police chief Danielle Fontaine is here with me. She'll work this case with us." Walsh provided a succinct recap of the events for his team. "EMS is on the way. HFTF will take the investigation lead, starting with the crime scene examination. Any evidence collected will go to the Iowa state lab to avoid conflict of interest, since Jayne is the GIPD evidence technician. Additionally, Skyler, manage all ballistics processing."

Dani bristled, then silently acquiesced to his judgment call.

Sirens screamed in the distance.

"Finally," Dani softly addressed Jayne, "Help's almost here."

"Please state your name when you speak for Chief Fontaine," Walsh directed.

"Eliana Kastell, tech specialist," the woman who'd answered said. "Elijah and Graham are the closest to your location."

"Eliana's system provides real-time GPS for the members," Walsh explained to Dani.

"ETA 10 minutes," a man said. "Sorry, DEA agent Graham Kenyon."

Knox whined, his gaze flitting between the back of the warehouse and Dani.

Walsh jerked his chin, getting her attention.

"What's up?" Dani whispered, stroking the dog's ears.

"Good," Walsh said. "Kenyon twins, take the lead on the evidence handling, especially recording the chain of custody, and secure the transfer to the Iowa state lab."

"Officer Elijah Kenyon," another man replied. "Won't Nebraska have a problem with that?"

"I'll notify them of the conflict of interest within this internal investigation," Walsh answered.

"ATF agent Skyler Rios," a woman said. "You've confirmed the missing weapon?"

"Yes," Walsh responded.

Skyler added, "I'll send all ballistics to my NIBIN contact and advise it's an urgent request."

Dani recognized the reference to the National Integrated Ballistic Information Network. An inside connection expedited processing.

Knox nudged Dani's arm. "Shh." She stroked his scruff.

"The rest of you assemble at the Rock by midnight," Walsh ordered.

A chorus of "Roger that" and "Affirmative" bounced over the line before he disconnected.

"What's the Rock?" Dani asked.

"Our Omaha headquarters." He glanced at Knox. "Is something wrong with him?"

The K-9 whined, again nudging Dani's arm. "Oh, sorry, sweetie, I didn't realize I still had your leash attached to me." She wriggled free of the lead and the dog scurried off, nose to the ground.

Walsh and Dani exchanged confused glances, then followed Knox to the far side of the building, where he disappeared into a hallway.

Dani ran to catch up and spotted a tall stack of boxes concealing a door.

Was the shooter still there?

Based on the increased siren decibels, reinforcements were closer. Walsh withdrew his weapon again. They shoved aside the boxes, revealing the sign that read Janitor's Closet.

A strange mewing, comparable to a cat's late-night cries, rose from the gap beneath the door. Knox scratched at the entry and the howls intensified, competing with the sirens outside.

"What's making that noise?" Dani tried the handle. "It's locked."

"May I?" Walsh's hulking size and muscular frame hadn't diminished over the years. If anyone could break down the door, it'd be him.

She stepped aside, and he rushed forward, shoulder-first.

It didn't budge, and he winced.

Dani peered closer. Steel. No wonder.

Remembering the key in Jayne's palm, Dani said, "Wait here." She spun on her heel and sprinted to the main warehouse, retrieved the key, then hurried back to Walsh.

They flanked the entrance, guns at the ready, and Dani unlocked the door, then nudged it open.

Dani gasped, dropping to her knees. "Oh, no." She lifted Jayne's distraught six-month-old daughter from the carrier. "Tessa." Cradling her, she asked, "What's a fugitive and a missing weapon got to do with Jayne and Tessa?"

"Apparently," Walsh replied, "everything."

# TWO

Dani paced the Rock several hours later as HFTF worked the case. The infant's feathery hair tickled her cheek as she cradled and patted Tessa's back. The baby hadn't enjoyed the extended ride to Omaha. To Walsh's credit, he'd not complained, and Knox had done his best to comfort Tessa. She'd found his fur intriguing, making the last forty minutes of the commute bearable.

HFTF's K-9s sprawled around the room, peering up as she passed by them. Walsh had introduced her to his team, whom he was clearly proud of, and they'd all been welcoming.

"You should be in bed," Dani whispered against Tessa's tiny ear.

Walsh held her gaze with an I-told-you-so look. She'd pleaded with him to delay the transfer to Child Protective Services the entire drive. He'd agreed only because it wasn't a violation of protocol since Jayne was injured, not deceased. Her heart refused to transfer the baby into a stranger's care. She'd promised Jayne that she'd look after Tessa. She intended to keep that promise. Whatever it took. And guilt for not protecting Jayne weighed on Dani. Until they received confirmation Jayne would recover, she wanted Tessa close.

"Need help?" Eliana Kastell, HFTF's computer technician, asked from her seated position at the kidney-shaped table. Auburn strands had escaped her messy bun, and even at the late hour her green eyes were bright.

Dani had instantly taken to the woman. "Is she asleep?" She turned slowly, allowing Eliana to see the baby's face.

"Yep, she's out." Eliana leaned back, revealing her pregnant belly.

"Eliana, go home and rest." ATF agent Skyler Rios slid into the chair beside her. Walsh had told Dani on the ride over of his plan to train Skyler to be his successor.

She assessed the agent, who oozed strength and professionalism. Her dark hair was pulled in a severe ponytail, accentuating the narrow lines of her face. Her intense gaze and no-nonsense manner testified to Skyler's capability.

Deputy US marshal Riker Kastell leaned toward Eliana and kissed his wife's cheek. "That's what I told her."

The group's easy communication style and kindness impressed Dani.

"No way, I'm in my second trimester and feeling great." Eliana shifted her computer, giving Skyler elbow room.

Dani slid into a chair.

"We're grateful for your help." Walsh stood before the evidence board, which was covered in pictures, maps, and information.

"Dani, any update on Jayne?" FBI agent Tiandra Daugherty asked.

"She's out of surgery, but still in critical condition." Dani's throat constricted.

"We're praying for her," Deputy US marshal Chance Tavalla replied.

Two men entered the room carrying large boxes that they placed on the table. Dani did a double-take. Except for their clothing, the men were identical. One wore jeans and a black pullover. The other, dark cargo pants and a light T-shirt with the HFTF logo on the right pocket.

The team distributed coffee and sandwiches.

"Figured you needed fuel." The man in the dark cargo pants extended his hand to Dani. "Officer Elijah Kenyon."

She shook his proffered hand. "Chief Dani Fontaine."

"Pleased to meet you, ma'am."

The second man pushed Elijah aside good-naturedly, shaking Dani's hand. "DEA agent Graham Kenyon. And, no, you're not seeing double. I'm the better-looking one."

"I wondered if I was hallucinating," she teased.

"Do I get combat pay for riding with him?" Elijah pointed at his twin.

"Graham's driving is horrendous," Tiandra said, revealing a slight southern accent filled with playfulness. The FBI agent jerked a chin toward Graham.

"Right?" Elijah consumed a section of the wall with his massive six-foot-one-inch muscular frame. "He gives me heartburn."

"I'm a trained professional," Graham replied, narrowing his gray-blue eyes at his twin.

Dani appreciated their light chitchat, but her raw emotions contrasted with the aromas, upsetting her stomach. "I'll take a coffee, please."

Tiandra passed her a cup.

"Thanks," Dani said. "Whatever Jayne intended to share tonight was important enough to warrant privacy."

Tiandra extended her long legs out and crossed her ankles. "Why endanger Tessa?"

"She put her in the closet to protect her," Dani countered defensively, knowing her friend wouldn't have let Tessa come to harm.

Riker shook his head. "Wouldn't a sitter be a smarter choice?" He addressed Dani, pinning her with his blue eyes.

"Tessa is in full-time day care. Jayne picks her up right after her shift ends. She hates being away from her baby."

Compassion filled Eliana's emerald irises. "GIPD's video footage confirmed Jayne left work at 1700."

"That's a considerable unaccounted window between then and our arrival at the warehouse," Walsh noted.

Skyler leaned forward. "Any progress finding a relative to care for Tessa?"

"None," Eliana said. "Jayne's mother passed two years ago, and her personnel documents list Dani as her emergency contact."

Her friend's trust in Dani left her speechless.

"What about Tessa's father?" Walsh asked.

"He died after Jayne learned she was pregnant." Tessa nestled against Dani and the scent of baby lotion wafted to her.

Her developing friendship with Jayne apparently lacked details. They'd discussed their present or future dreams, not their histories.

"There's gotta be someone," Dani protested.

"We'll keep searching," Eliana assured her.

Dani thoughtfully contemplated her next words. "I promised Jayne that I would take care of Tessa should anything happen to her."

Understanding quietly passed through the group.

"Broken Bow PD is unhappy with us for taking over the shooting investigation at the warehouse." Walsh sighed, redirecting the discussion. "I smoothed things over, but tread lightly."

"Can't blame them," Riker responded. "We rolled into their jurisdictional wheelhouse and took over."

"We don't want to open Pandora's worms." Walsh confused the two clichés. "Don't release details of the intersecting investigations."

"Knowledge is power. Only NSP could usurp us," Elijah replied, referencing the Nebraska State Patrol.

"I pulled a lot of strings, favors, and basically promised my ranch for their permission to work this case," Walsh reminded the group.

The man she remembered would've never gone through all that trouble to help her. Dani's gaze lingered on Walsh. Flickers of gray added to the attractiveness of his sandy brown hair. His brown eyes were soft and inviting, and his muscular physique hadn't diminished over the years either. Walsh's strong demeanor exceeded his handsomeness. Humbled, she said, "I appreciate all you're doing."

"Crime scene processing was minimal except for the casings," Graham advised. "It's all bagged and logged into the Iowa crime lab."

"Let's address the obvious elephant we're avoiding." Walsh sat opposite Dani.

She'd noticed his distancing all evening. Not that it surprised her, considering their decades-long estrangement. Had he told his team about their falling out? No, when would he? They'd been together since the warehouse shooting.

Memories of their past flittered to mind. Walsh's investigation into Cortez PD Chief Varmose, then Dani's boss, had destroyed she and Walsh's relationship. If he'd told her what he was doing, instead of hiding the case and his role, they might've had a chance. Or not.

Yes, she'd missed Chief Varmose's corruption until it was too late. But in her defense, she'd also been a rookie cop, brand new to Cortez PD. Wasn't loyalty to the brotherhood part of the job? She'd stuck to her guns, believing the best about Varmose, and proved herself committed to her agency and her commander. Until Walsh had presented the undisputable evidence against the chief, simultaneously making her the scapegoat to the rest of her co-workers. Their disdain and assumption that Dani was involved in the sting had almost cost her everything.

Tonight, Walsh had striven to help her. She appreciated his efforts, while reasoning he owed her that much after nearly destroying her career years prior. She was at Beckham Walsh's mercy, but they weren't friends. Detachment from him was fine.

"The GIPD-compromised evidence—specifically the Smith & Wesson 9 mm pistol directly linked to the multi-jurisdictional weapons trafficking takedown involving Enrique Prachank—" Walsh began "—is crucial. We're all aware of the critical need to recover that ASAP."

Dani averted her eyes, staring at the tabletop.

"I have concerns regarding any other evidence we stored at GIPD," Walsh said.

Like salt in a painful wound, Dani winced at the implication.

"That being said," he continued, "Dani will work with us to determine the item and system breakdown."

Expecting condemnation and judgment in their eyes, Dani forced herself to look up. Not one person offered a harsh glance. Inhaling a fortifying breath, she said, "I'm confident there's a logical explanation. Since Jayne cannot assist us, we're on our own to discover those details."

"We'll conduct this investigation with no special treatment, shortcuts, or favoritism. Jayne's participation and/or responsibility is obviously a tremendous concern."

Dani stiffened. His comment reiterated her view of the real Beckham Walsh.

She'd never leave Jayne's future in the hands of this über-focused egomaniac. Walsh ignored allegiances, satisfying his ambitions, regardless of the fallout. He'd proved himself in that respect, and he'd never blindside her again.

"Dani, are you familiar with the case Walsh referenced?" Tiandra asked.

"The bare bones."

"Mastermind criminal Enrique Prachank established and controlled an underground arms and drug dealing network spanning South Dakota, Nebraska, and Iowa. He trafficked weapons of both legal and illegal varieties," Tiandra said. "We tied one of his guns to multiple murders. It's the key evidence we have against him."

"Like taking down Capone with tax evasion instead of his other crimes," Dani postulated.

"Right. You take what you can get," Skyler replied. "The murder charges will earn him life in prison."

Elijah leaned forward. "We have to sever the head of the snake, or they'll just resume their activities."

"He's a fugitive, correct?" Dani asked.

"Yes. Prachank's been on the run for over a year. He's also our priority case." Chance stroked his German shepherd, Destiny. "Grand Island PD is one of the contracted off-sight evidence storage locations."

"It's all negotiated in our multi-agency memorandums of understanding," Walsh inserted.

Dani was aware of the agreements, but she didn't interrupt.

Chance nodded. "Prachank's gotta have the missing weapon."

"Find that and you'll find him," Dani concluded.

"Jayne asked us to meet her at the location." Walsh redirected.

"Technically, she called me," Dani argued. "Obviously, she assumed the warehouse was safe."

Walsh's frigid stare corrected her. She wasn't mulling the facts with the perspective of an investigator.

"I'm sorry, go on."

"She might've lured you there." Graham munched on a sandwich.

"Assuming that's true. What's Jayne's motive?" Riker addressed Dani, "Did you have an argument? Any reason she'd want revenge or retribution?"

The group pinned Riker with shaking heads. "What?" He lifted his hands in surrender. "It's a valid question."

"Riker battled his own brother's vengeance," Tiandra explained. "His thoughts start with that intention."

The details sparked hope in Dani. If they'd each faced personal challenges, surely, they'd have compassion on Jayne's. "I saw Jayne three weeks ago at church. We always meet for breakfast after service. Kind of a tradition. We had a pleasant conversation about nothing in particular," Dani said. "She doesn't report directly to me. Additionally, I've been out of town at a conference for over a week. Just got back today."

"Did she seem distraught?" Chance asked.

Dani shook her head. She and Jayne's single relationship status had bonded their friendship.

"Is she dating?" Skyler questioned.

"No, she's focused on her daughter." Dani considered the way Jayne doted on Tessa.

"She's balancing a full-time job with parenting," Eliana surmised.

"An impossible task. Something takes a backseat." Dani regretted the words immediately.

"Might explain the evidence issues," Elijah agreed.

Great, she'd added fuel to the fire.

"Monday, we'll interview her coworkers," Graham advised.

"It's late." Walsh stacked his files. "Recoup over the weekend."

"Technically, it is Saturday," Eliana said good-naturedly.

Walsh nodded. "Right. Take the rest of today and Sunday off. Then tackle your assignments, and we'll reconvene on Monday. Dani, HFTF has a small condo here in Omaha. You're welcome to stay there."

"Thank you." She'd dreaded making the two-hour return trip to Grand Island.

The group stood and huddled, offering prayers for wisdom, for protection over Tessa, and for Jayne's healing. Dani's chest tightened with humility and appreciation as their collective amens filled the room.

She glanced at the baby. "I have nothing for Tessa except her carrier and what's in the diaper bag."

"Brilliant thinking to grab the carrier's car seat base. That's essential. You can borrow the playpen we have," Eliana offered, glancing at Riker. "Our little one won't need it for a few more months." She stroked her belly in a nurturing and protective manner.

"Thank you." Overwhelmed with gratitude, Dani blinked away tears. What was wrong with her? The late hour and chain of events were playing on her emotions.

"I'll bring it over," Riker offered.

"Oh, and I'll add in some other must-haves for you," Eliana added.

"You all are amazing." Dani forced down the lump in her throat.

"It's what family does." Tiandra gave her shoulder a squeeze.

The group dispersed along with their dogs, leaving her alone with Walsh.

"I'll give you a ride to the condo," he said.

"I hate to move her." Dani brushed her cheek against Tessa's soft skin. "But we both need sleep."

"Agreed…" Walsh hesitated.

Dani tilted her head. "What's up?"

"You won't want to hear this, but—"

"Jayne wasn't involved in anything underhanded," Dani cut him off. "Tessa was her life. She'd never willfully endanger her."

"Reconsider Child Protective Services assuming temporary custody. They'll keep Tessa safe and allow you to focus on the case."

Dani glared at him. "I promised Jayne I would ensure Tessa was protected and cared for. I can't just hand her over to strangers, regardless of their qualifications." Especially not after almost getting her mother killed.

Whatever it took, Dani would keep her promise to Jayne and be Tessa's caregiver until she recovered. And, she had to prove Jayne's innocence and arrest the shooter. The one question she couldn't answer was what Jayne had tried to tell her before the incident. That information could've cost their lives.

Worse, Dani had a feeling the danger wasn't gone.

Walsh led the way to his SUV, helping Knox into the kennel while Dani settled Tessa's carrier into the car seat base they'd retrieved from Jayne's car at the warehouse. Her movements spoke of experience. He wondered about her personal life since their breakup all those years ago. She'd apparently done all right for herself after leaving Cortez PD. Regret for how he'd handled the investigation into her then chief, Varmose, and the man's subsequent conviction still stung. Walsh had never meant to hurt Dani, yet he'd done exactly that. As one of the investigators, he couldn't risk his career by warning her ahead of time. She'd never forgiven him for blindsiding her.

He'd only been doing his job.

His ambition preceded all. That was what a good cop did. Wasn't that the excuse he'd given when he'd failed to protect those he'd cared for? First Dani, then his deceased wife, Gwen.

Recently, Walsh wondered whether he'd misplaced his loyalties. Once he retired, the marshals would replace him without a second thought. His commitment had cost him everything, and he'd have nothing to show for it in the end.

Not even his law enforcement identity.

What did he have besides his job?

All the could've been's lingered in his mind. His and Dani's relationship had started out wonderfully, but it never got beyond the new stage, thanks to Walsh's career pursuits.

Dani's fierce loyalties were unwavering. Regardless of the evidence against Varmose, she'd exploded at Walsh, touting her boyfriend had used her to get information on the captain while blindsiding her to the aftermath. She'd ended their relationship. Rightly so.

His career had soared after that, permitting him to deliberately evade any close connection with her. He focused on cases geographically distanced from central Nebraska, only recently learning about Dani's promotion to GIPD.

She faced him. "Why are you looking at me like that?"

Walsh blinked, searching for an explanation to divert the conversation, and blurted, "You're a natural." He swallowed. "With the baby."

"I've spent time with Tessa, so I'm familiar with what works to calm her down."

She offered nothing more and Walsh took the hint. Right. Better to sustain a professional relationship. Asking her personal questions led to the reverse. A vulnerability he'd not return if the conversation focused on him.

His failures had morphed Walsh into a loner with

too many regrets. That was nobody's business. He glanced at Tessa before closing the door. All his dreams of a happily-ever-after family had died with his wife, Gwen. He'd missed the opportunity for a normal life, devoting himself to law enforcement. Soon, that would mean nothing. The fear of his uncharted future pricked at him. Only four years remained before his mandatory retirement from the marshals.

Dani shut her passenger door and he slid in behind the wheel, starting the engine.

Their conversation dwindled on the drive to the condo—a recent acquisition for housing HFTF witnesses.

Once they reached the property, Walsh parked, and they exited the vehicle.

Approaching lights demanded their attention.

Dani set the carrier down, then drew her gun.

Walsh stepped closer, exhaling relief at the sight of the familiar pickup. "It's Riker. Go ahead, and I'll help him carry in stuff."

"Come on, Knox." Dani and the Dobie mix ascended the exterior staircase to the second-level unit.

Walsh maintained a visual on them while walking to Riker.

"Sorry, would've been here sooner, but Eliana kept adding things for Dani." Riker chuckled, opening the back door.

They withdrew several bags and a strange rectangular object.

"It's a Pack 'n Play," Riker explained.

Walsh grunted. His military and law enforcement experience had instilled skills and training to handle dangerous equipment and situations. But the unfamiliar baby contraptions Riker hauled to the apartment baffled him.

Dani held open the door while they carried in the load. Riker set up the Pack 'n Play and Walsh helped Dani unpack the bags. "Eliana also threw in some extra clothes and supplies for you as well."

Dani blinked. "Thank you."

"You've got enough for twenty babies." Walsh handed her a package of diapers.

"Unfortunately, we'll go through those fast," Dani replied. "Bless Eliana! She thought of everything." She held up two large bottles. "Baby wash and lotion."

Tessa grunted from her carrier. Dani changed the infant into strange pajamas with no leg holes and mittens over her hands, then transferred her to the playpen.

"Doesn't she need blankets and a pillow?" Walsh asked.

Based upon Riker and Dani's dumfounded expressions, the answer was no.

"Alrighty." Walsh withdrew his keys. The universal sign for *I'm leaving.* "Take tomorrow, er, the remainder of today and Sunday. I'll pick you up at 0900 Monday."

"Thanks," Dani replied. "I should've driven my vehicle. I'm sorry to impose on you."

"No problem," Walsh assured.

"Please extend my appreciation to Eliana for everything." Dani accompanied them to the door.

"Will do. Night." Riker turned and jogged down the steps to the parking lot.

"Walsh," Dani said.

He faced her. "Yeah."

"I won't deny my friendship with Jayne affects me." She glanced over her shoulder at the playpen. "Based on the team meeting, it sounds as if you've fought personal battles without compromising your integrity. I'm no exception."

He'd witnessed Dani's unrelenting loyalty that blinded her to reality once before with her old chief, Varmose. Though she'd come around to accepting the truth about the man's corrupt involvement after Walsh had provided evidence. Yet that stubborn streak returned, and it appeared they were on the same opposing sides again.

"Jayne was in trouble or had found something significant. She'd never endanger Tessa." Dani wrapped herself in a hug.

Walsh shoved his hands into his pockets, torn between wanting to comfort her and wanting to scream at her delusional reasoning. Jayne was guilty and involved. He just didn't have the evidence. Yet.

"She hasn't always made the best choices, from the little of her past she shared," Dani justified. "However, she lives for Tessa. Give me time to learn why this happened."

Walsh glimpsed at the baby resting in the playpen. His heart extended to the innocent caught in this mess, but it changed nothing. If Jayne was guilty, he'd arrest her.

"Get some sleep. We'll talk more later." He turned without another look at Dani, inhaling the humid summer night air.

The door closed softly, and he sighed. Their brief reunion rekindled familiar and unwanted emotions. Losing Dani had devastated him, but it had never diminished his feelings for her, professionally and personally.

That was his job as a commander, and he felt the same for her as he did all the HFTF staff.

*Liar.* The thought assailed him, and he flinched.

Dani was different. She'd invaded his heart in ways he'd never imagined possible. She was like no other woman he'd ever known. Dani had strength and intelligence that had skyrocketed her in their academy days. Her slender, lean build masked the physical capabilities she possessed. They'd competed without issue, becoming fast friends before their budding romance. But when Dani looked at Walsh, he felt his knees grow weak and his pulse race. She still took his breath away. And, truthfully, he feared his inability to remain impartial to her.

He descended the steps to the ground level. Dani might be right about Jayne, but his instincts said otherwise. He intended to uncover the truth about the woman. Nobody endangered those he cared for and got away with it. He'd put whoever had attacked them at the warehouse behind bars and expose Jayne's involvement.

A flicker in the distance grabbed his attention.

Walsh surveyed the landscape. Had he imagined it? He stepped back, looking up at Dani's apartment door. No light glowed from her unit's windows.

Had the shooter followed them to this location?

For a moment, Walsh considered moving Dani and Tessa.

Another visual of the area and he spotted only cars parked in the lot and the slight breeze fluttering the leaves of the trees.

They'd spent hours at the Rock before driving here. He was hypervigilant. Besides, if she'd gotten Tessa to sleep, he didn't want to wake them over nothing.

Resolved, he returned to the SUV. Sliding into the driver's seat, he withdrew his binoculars and scanned the surroundings.

His breath hitched at the motion of a person shifting between parked cars in the neighboring housing development. Homing in on a black-clad figure drawing closer, he shut off the SUV's overhead light, snagged his gun and exited the vehicle.

He started for the intruder, keeping to the shadows, and moved to the main apartment building. As he neared the first-floor window of a unit, a dog barked, then pawed at the glass.

Walsh ducked behind a bush, spying the figure bolting in the opposite direction.

"Stop!" Walsh disregarded his surreptitious approach and gave chase.

He lost sight of the person after he dodged between

two trucks parked beside a fence. Was it a car thief or burglar? Or had he come for Dani?

Furious, Walsh spun on his heel and stormed to his SUV, resolved to stay and provide protection detail. With too many unanswered questions, he couldn't risk leaving Dani and Tessa unattended. He considered notifying Dani, but knew he'd only wake her if necessary. However, he'd involve Chance and Graham. They'd take shifts in the hope the intruder returned.

If he did, Walsh vowed he'd not escape again.

# THREE

Monday morning arrived too soon. Even with Sunday to rest, minus a trip to the ER to ensure Tessa was all right after the warehouse incident, Dani hadn't fully recuperated from the shooting late on Friday. She had spent the morning checking in at GIPD, ensuring she was only a phone call away should her staff need to reach her. Walsh's SUV pulled into the parking lot. His attempt at surreptitious security detail hadn't worked. She'd seen him, Chance, and Graham performing shifts outside the condo over the weekend. Her heart warmed at their concern for her and Tessa.

Tessa's bags sat by the door. Walsh hadn't contacted her, and she chalked up the exterior protection as his overcautious quirk.

Knox squeaked out a yawn, causing Dani's chain reaction response. She stretched her back, then offered him a scratch between the ears. "You're tired too."

Unaware of Tessa's normal schedule, she couldn't tell if the baby regularly slept in short three-hour increments. Maybe the unfamiliar bed affected her. Each time Tessa fussed, Dani and Knox awoke with her. She'd not complain, at least not to Walsh. He'd made his intention of putting Tessa in Child Protective Services clear and Dani refused to encourage that notion. She'd survived on less rest during her undercover ops. Of course, that was ten years prior.

Once more, respect for Jayne's life as a single mom had Dani praying for her friend. How had she worked full-time with regular intervals of limited sleep? She'd never heard Jayne whine. "Please heal her, Lord," Dani prayed aloud. She'd called the hospital several times, but Jayne's condition hadn't changed.

Dani feared the worst.

Knox glanced up from the bed as though in agreement with the petition.

Tessa let out a howl, and Dani lifted her from the playpen. "Good morning, darling." She rubbed the infant's back. "I know, you're missing your mama."

Dani walked to the kitchen and completed mixing Tessa's formula, then sat to feed her. The doorbell rang, and she readjusted, cradling the infant in one arm, and hurried to open the door.

"Morning." Walsh extended a drink carrier containing two cardboard cups. His gaze bounced from her to Tessa, then at the drinks, before he retracted the offer.

"Sorry, I'm short a hand," Dani joked. "Come in."

She turned and walked back to the chair she'd previously abandoned. He followed, pulled out a seat opposite her and withdrew the coffee. "I wasn't sure what you'd like. I have one plain black brew and a vanilla latte."

"Oh, the latte, please." She reconsidered. "Unless you wanted that."

"Not a chance." He passed her the cup marked with a big V on the side.

Dani glimpsed her reflection in the decorative mirror over the couch and winced. "I'm running behind."

She still needed to shower and dress. She'd pinned her hair in a messy bun, and she wore the sweats and an oversize T-shirt Eliana had provided.

"It's okay. I'm early, so I'll make calls while you're getting ready." Walsh's cell phone rang. "Case in point." He smiled, revealing the handsomeness Dani had tried to ignore before.

She blinked and averted her eyes. Sleep deprivation made her wonky.

"Morning, Skyler," Walsh answered on speakerphone. "I'm here with Dani."

*"Hola,"* the chipper ATF agent responded. "I'm visiting my *abuela* this month and need to practice my Spanish to impress her."

Walsh chuckled. "Whatever works to bring us her amazing tamales."

"Definitely. I've got news."

"Hopefully good?" Dani asked.

"Not exactly. My NIBIN contact called this morning. The ballistics evidence recovered from the warehouse shooting came back as a match already logged in the system."

"How's that possible?" Dani asked. Then it hit her. The gun had been used in a previous investigation. She sat straighter. "You have my full attention."

Tessa wriggled, frustrated, and a small wail escaped as she readjusted the bottle.

*"Hola,* Tessa," Skyler said.

"Sorry, we're multitasking here," Dani explained.

"No worries."

"Go ahead," Walsh prompted.

"The casings matched a Smith & Wesson 9 mm collected in the Enrique Prachank case."

"The missing firearm our team logged into the GIPD evidence locker with the rest of the weapons cache after the takedown. Prachank's compelling, literally smoking, gun," Walsh concluded.

*"Sí jefe,"* Skyler said.

"What?" Walsh asked.

"Yes, boss," Skyler translated.

Dani blinked, staring at the phone, thoughts racing. "But that makes no sense."

"Trust me, it's legit. Ran it three times," Skyler replied. "I don't have to tell you the mess this opens."

"It's the first connection we've had on Prachank since he escaped custody," Walsh said. "Notify the rest of the team."

"Okay. That gun tied him to several homicides," Skyler added, as though Dani needed the reminder. "Without it, Prachank's lawyer has a chance of getting his case thrown out for insufficient evidence."

The same weapon Jayne was responsible to secure as part of her job.

"We'll be in the office shortly," Walsh said.

"Roger that."

They disconnected.

Dani excused herself to finish feeding Tessa in the bedroom, while Walsh made phone calls.

"Help me out, kiddo." The baby grunted her disagreement, melting into tears as Dani settled her in the carrier. "You asked for it." Dani belted out an '80s song, and Tessa quieted. Poor kid probably wanted her to stop, but it worked.

She got ready faster than she had during her academy days as her mind raced with the implications of Skyler's call.

Within ten minutes, she finished, whipping her hair into a ponytail. She hauled Tessa in her carrier—occupied with a stuffed elephant—to the living room and placed her beside Walsh. His expression shifted between amusement and intimidation as he looked at the baby. Had something happened? Was he debating Prachank's situation against Jayne's involvement…or did infants make him uncomfortable?

She stifled a giggle. "Babies not your thing?" She retrieved Tessa.

"Uh, haven't been around them much." She'd never seen Walsh appear anything other than confident in any circumstance. But when he beheld Tessa, his forehead creased, and he appeared conflicted.

"Ready?" Walsh seemed eager to leave as he hurried to the door.

"As I'll ever be," she responded, picking up the carrier.

"What can I haul out for you?"

"Grab that," Dani said, gesturing with her free hand toward the purple diaper bag by the door.

"Want the playpen too?"

She considered the request. "Probably not a bad idea."

Walsh walked to the Pack 'n Play and stood looking down at it. "Do I need a degree in engineering to fold it?"

She smiled. "No worries, I've got it." Dani put Tessa down, then with a few quick movements, she'd folded the playpen.

"It's a giant origami project," Walsh teased.

Dani laughed a little too hard. She gave herself a mental slap upside the head. "Lack of sleep is affecting me." Why had she confessed that?

"Did she keep you up?" Walsh glanced at Tessa.

"No problem," Dani insisted, hoisting the carrier. "C'mon, Knox, time to work."

The Dobie mix stretched out his lanky legs and slowly got to his feet, and they trailed Walsh to his SUV.

"If I hauled her around every day, I could eliminate some of my upper body workouts," she quipped. "After the meeting, would you mind driving me to GI later today to pick up my vehicle?" She used the initials for Grand Island, as most Nebraskans did.

"Sure, but I don't have a problem chauffeuring you," Walsh assured her. "It's nice to have the company."

Dani doubted he felt that way, but she didn't comment.

"In fact—" he glanced at his watch "—let's get on the road now. I'll update the team on our plans." They finished loading Tessa and Knox. The dog leaned closer to the infant, guarding her. "Good boy, Knox."

Once they were moving, she said, "We need to talk about the newest elephant between us."

As though in response to her words, Tessa let out a

wail of disapproval. His gaze flicked to the rearview mirror as he dialed his team using his hands-free device and updated them of his plan to take Dani to GI. Rather than take Tessa on the four-hour roundtrip and to the station, Eliana agreed to watch her at the Rock. Dani hated leaving her, but headquarters would be the safest place for her while they continued investigating—starting with the evidence room.

After a few moments of silence, Dani said, "I can guess what you're thinking." She shifted uncomfortably in the seat.

"I've got no doubt."

"There's a reasonable explanation and we'll find it," she told him confidently.

"Jayne is the GIPD evidence technician responsible for Prachank's gun," Walsh replied. "There's no coincidence here."

"He's a fugitive," Dani contended. "We've got no proof Jayne stole it from the locker."

"That's the likeliest scenario," Walsh argued.

She hesitated. Her internal cop self agreed with Walsh. The implications against Jayne were strong. But Dani refused to believe her friend would risk her career and her baby to help a criminal. Still, she needed a justifiable argument with validity, not feelings, to persuade Walsh.

"Prachank has connections. There's a reason he's eluded capture all this time. It's conceivable he paid someone on the inside to get the gun for him. Without it, the state will have trouble prosecuting. It's crucial proof against him. His freedom is his strongest motive for getting that weapon back."

"True. And his scumbag lawyer could've suggested or even helped Prachank line up the theft, since he's harped most on the fact that the weapon is the only evidence against Prachank. Eliminate it, and the rest teeters off balance," Walsh stated. "He could be mocking us. Not only was he able to get it out of the evidence locker, but he plans to keep using it."

"Yeah." Dani sighed. "Except why do something as foolish as shooting at us with the gun he stole? It practically advertises he has it."

"Desperation," Walsh replied. "It has the power to convince even the smartest people to make poor decisions."

Dani couldn't agree more. And she was determined to prove Jayne hadn't stolen the firearm.

Finally, on the road after transferring Tessa into the team's care at the Rock, Walsh and Dani were on the highway. He'd silently considered the situation with Prachank's weapons, and concluded they had to first question the fugitive's attorney.

Walsh slid on his sunglasses, shielding his eyes against the late-morning sun that pierced the windshield.

"It's going to be a hot one today," he said.

"Supposed to be record highs all week," Dani replied.

They were discussing the weather? How pathetic was that? But he struggled to talk with her. She'd not come out and argued with him regarding the implications of Jayne stealing evidence. However, Walsh understood the depth of Dani's devotions. They'd fought this battle once before and it had ended their relationship. Now they were in a similar position. He didn't want to repeat the same mistakes this time. But he'd been correct all those years ago about her boss, Varmose, and the corruption he'd dragged into Cortez PD that Walsh had unveiled.

And he felt certain he was on target about Jayne.

Dani's reason for withholding her defense argument was more than the words. He again debated removing her from the investigation. She was too invested. They couldn't jeopardize the case, for Dani's sake.

In Walsh's experience, he'd learned the best people could still make the wrong choices for the right reasons.

He agreed with her on some points, though. What had made Jayne desperate enough to risk prison, her livelihood, and losing custody of her daughter? Those questions remained his focus regardless of Jayne's relationship with Dani. He was the commander of the Heartland Fugitive Task Force. If necessary, he'd pull rank and remove Dani from the investigation, prepared for the battle that he'd face with her.

"Aren't we going to GI?" Dani asked, interrupting his thoughts.

He winced, merged onto Highway 81 and headed north, realizing he'd not shared his intentions with her. "I apologize. I'm working through everything in my mind and neglected to share."

"Regarding what, exactly?"

"Change of plans. It's a reasonable assumption someone with insider knowledge and capability stole the gun from Grand Island PD's evidence room. Regardless of the motive, I want to talk to Prachank's lawyer first."

"You think he's behind this?"

"If anyone knows Prachank, it's his attorney," Walsh replied.

Dani withdrew her cell phone. "Should I call and demand he meet with us?"

"Nope. I prefer the advantage of surprise."

"Works for me." She settled back in her seat. "So, who is this illustrious lawyer, and where does the bottom dweller work?"

He chuckled at her silliness. "Raymond Strauss resides outside of Humphrey, under a different name. Though his office address is in Omaha, even he doesn't want his clients to know where he lives. If that tells you the type of clientele he services."

"Wow, no kidding."

Walsh flipped on the air conditioner, and Knox peered through the divider, soaking it up. Walsh used one hand to pet him.

He turned off the highway onto the county road. They traversed the rolling hills, typical of northeastern Nebraska, toward the small town of Humphrey.

They rounded a pivot corner, spotting a house and barn. The loud whirring of a bright red motorcycle gained his attention. The driver and passenger were both clad completely in black-leather gear, with full helmets and darkened face shields.

"They have to be baking in those clothes," Walsh said.

Dani twisted around.

The motorcyclist revved the engine and Walsh got a better glimpse of the newer model Kawasaki Ninja. "Fast ride."

Emphasizing Walsh's evaluation, the bike screeched and did a slingshot to the left. The red blur zipped past Walsh on the driver's side.

"What an idiot," he muttered.

"Yeah. I'd charge him with excessive display of acceleration," Dani confirmed.

"And reckless driving." Walsh shook his head.

"I'm calling him into the state patrol." Dani withdrew her cell phone, and he listened as she reported the bike.

The Kawasaki disappeared by the time she'd finished.

"They'll be watching for him."

"Doubt they'll catch him, though," Walsh argued. "Those guys know how to dodge the authorities, and there are plenty of side roads for them to disappear."

"Well, aren't you Mr. Negative today," Dani quipped.

He frowned. "I'm pessimistic. There's a difference."

"If you say so." She chuckled.

The landscape transitioned into deeper rolling hills, surrounding them in acres of corn and soybean fields. The SUV crested the rising peaks of the road before plunging down into the valleys. "Being out here makes me want to get back to the ranch."

Dani quirked a brow. "Is that code for something?"

"No." Walsh guffawed. "Marissa and I own a rescue horse ranch near Ponca State Park."

"I haven't seen her in forever," Dani said, smiling. "How's she doing?"

Memories of the fire that nearly killed his sister only a short time ago assaulted him, instantly sobering Walsh. Strangely, it also reminded him how close danger had come to his family. He flicked a glance at Dani, empathizing with her worries for Jayne. "She was involved in a horrible attack when we were working a case. But she's fully recovered and back to her normal ornery self."

Dani grinned. "Don't you dare talk bad about her. I've always loved your baby sister. Does she still call you Becky?"

Walsh grimaced. "Yes. And don't try it."

"No guarantees." Dani laughed.

Walsh and Dani had met at the academy, becoming quick friends. It had taken him two years after they'd parted and started working in their respective departments to ask Dani out. Mainly thanks to Marissa's help. He'd forgotten the many dinners the trio had spent together before Walsh had exposed Varmose's drug dealing corruption in Dani's department. Sadness hovered with the bittersweet memories. "She's exactly as you remember her. Rescued another mare last week."

"You buy the horses, then resell them?" Dani asked.

"Nope. We provide forever homes at the ranch. Many were abused or neglected by their previous owners. Marissa and I give them a home where they're loved and cared for."

"That's cool. I'd love to see it sometime." The sincerity in her tone made him want to tell her more.

He wanted to prove to Dani that he wasn't the cold-hearted robot she'd once accused him of being. "We'll have to make it happen."

They settled into a comfortable silence.

How was it that decades had separated them, yet being around Dani still felt natural? As though they'd picked up right where they'd left off all those years ago?

The road narrowed as they approached a semi-truck hauling a massive load of hay bales.

"Well, we *were* making good time." Walsh decreased his speed. "Is it my imagination, or is that bale not secured up there?" He gestured toward the humungous, yellow roll of hay teetering ahead of them.

"They always look like that," Dani assured him. "Really, they're tightened down."

"Hmm," Walsh murmured, unconvinced. He prepared to pass the semi but was restricted by the No Passing road sign. "Makes me nervous watching a two-thousand-pound roll of hay rocking in front of me."

Ahead, the truck crept at a snail's pace up the steep hill with its weighted load. Walsh's gaze flicked forward where a shadowed figure inched atop the bales. "Is that—" His question was cut off by the distinct sound of a revving motorcycle engine screaming behind them.

"What's going on?" Dani twisted in her seat once again.

"Is that the same guy from earlier?" Walsh glanced in the side mirror, watching as the dark-clad figure drew closer, this time without a passenger.

Dani seemed to study the rider. "I'm not sure, but it doesn't look good."

Walsh unclipped his holster and withdrew his Glock, placing it beside him on the seat.

Dani also retrieved her gun and ordered, "Knox, down!" The dog immediately dove into the rear kennel.

The semi continued its painfully slow climb up the hill.

Blocked by the truck on the narrow uphill country road, where visibility was hindered by the semi's load, and the motorcycle behind them, they had nowhere to go.

Trapped.

The Kawasaki drew closer, and the driver hoisted an automatic rifle. He slung it across his chest, repositioned and aimed at the SUV.

Walsh's gaze flicked to the truck in front of them. There, he spotted the motorcycle's leather-clad passenger perched atop the bales, aiming an identical weapon at them.

"Get down!" he hollered, slamming into Park, then ducking in his seat as a barrage of bullets was unleashed upon them.

# FOUR

Glass rained in the SUV from the relentless gunfire. Dani and Walsh remained low while bullets pierced the seat cushions and interior just above Dani's head.

Then, as suddenly as it began, the shooting stopped. The motorcycle's engine revved as the bike sped away, leaving its screaming tires fading in the distance.

"Are you okay?" Walsh rose slowly, checking his surroundings.

"Yeah." Dani scooted up in her seat. "Knox, stay down!"

Still on the hill, the semi in front of them had come to a complete stop, its hazard lights flashing.

Walsh twisted around to see Knox. "Is he hurt?"

Dani leaned over the headrest, spotting her Dobie mix flat against the floorboards, thankfully unharmed. "No, he's fine." She reached out a hand to him. "Good job, Knox," she praised. "Stay." Dani didn't want her dog to cut his paws on the broken glass.

She turned, prepared to open her door, when a thud caught her attention. The massive two-thousand-pound bale of hay rocked.

As if in slow motion, the enormous bundle tumbled off the stack, barreling straight for Walsh's SUV.

"Down!" Walsh yelled.

Dani again slid to the floorboard as the bale crashed onto the hood of the SUV. The impact lifted the vehicle's back end, which remained suspended for a horribly long second before slamming down.

Dani's teeth rattled. Dirt, dust, and shards of hay filled the atmosphere. For several seconds, neither moved. She held her breath as the cloud of debris hindered her vision. Finally, she found her voice. "Walsh!"

"I'm here," he answered with a cough. "Are you okay?"

"Yes, I think so."

Walsh snagged his Glock from where it had fallen to the floorboard and Dani did the same. Both grunted with the effort of shoving open the vehicle doors, which were damaged but not demolished, and escaped the SUV.

Dani unlocked the kennel and the dog inched out of the rear passenger door, thankfully protected by the steel structure. He hopped down and gave a thorough shaking of his fur. She knelt beside Knox, running her hands over his short black coat. "Not a scratch." As though confirming her words, Knox lapped at her face. Dani chuckled. "I love you too." She snapped on his leash, keeping him close.

Dani took in the unbelievable sight of the supersize bale of hay caving the vehicle's hood. The semi remained still.

"Why did he stop?"

"I don't know." Walsh waved her to follow.

"Knox. Stay." The dog sat and Dani dropped the leash. "Stay," she reiterated.

With guns at the ready, they parted, each moving forward to approach the semi's cab.

The bales were wider than the vehicle, hiding the driver from view. Dani stayed with her back flat against the hay and inched closer. When she reached the front of the trailer, a wide grin crossed her face at the sight of the herd of cows meandering in the middle of the road.

Walsh rounded the semi too.

Her surprise at the bovines shifted when Walsh whispered, "Dani."

Her gaze roved to a section of plaid fabric fluttering in the breeze, apparently snagged on a break in the wire fence surrounding the pasture. Acres of cornstalks on the opposite side of the road beckoned the animals.

Dani raised her gun, prepared.

She glanced at Walsh, who brandished his Glock and stared ahead.

"Come out with your hands up!" Dani ordered, aiming her weapon at the field. "If you run, I will send my dog after you."

"Don't shoot!" a man wearing a red baseball cap called, emerging from the stalks.

A second man followed. He wore cowboy boots and a plaid shirt with a rip. Dani surmised it was the same fabric torn on the fence. He approached with his hands raised. "Please! Don't shoot."

"Come toward us. Slowly! Keep your hands above your head," Walsh ordered.

"Are you police?" the first asked.

"Yes," Dani replied, realizing she wore jeans and

a blouse while Walsh had on BDU pants and his uniform shirt. At least one of them looked professional.

Relief seemed to pour over the men's faces.

"Am I imagining that?" Dani asked under her breath.

"Nope, they're glad to see us," Walsh said before directing the men. "Stop where you are."

They halted in place, two feet from Dani and Walsh.

"Are you carrying any weapons?" Walsh questioned.

"No, sir," both replied in chorus.

"We need to check for our safety," Dani said.

The men turned, hands still above their heads, allowing Dani and Walsh to search them. Satisfied, they stepped back, holstering their weapons.

"You may lower your hands," Walsh said. They did as instructed, but apprehension covered their faces.

Dani whistled for Knox and the dog raced to her side, leash trailing. "Good boy."

He sat beside her, focused on the strangers.

She addressed the ball-cap-wearing man as he was closest to her. "Do you have identification?"

Both men warily gawked at Knox while reaching to retrieve their wallets from their back pockets. Walsh collected and studied the IDs before passing them to Dani.

"Vinson Jessup," Dani spoke to the ball cap wearer.

"Yes, ma'am. Are you all right?" Jessup replied.

She blinked, confused by the question.

"Were you hurt by the bale or the shooters?" the

second, whose driver's license read Timothy Bartle, reiterated.

"No. What happened to your shirt?" Dani asked Timothy.

He glanced down. "I don't know."

"We heard the gunshots and bolted out of the truck," Jessup explained.

"Then we saw the trailer rock and realized a bale had rolled off," Timothy added.

"Why did you stop?" Walsh asked.

"The cows," Jessup said.

"Were you aware a person was on the hay bales?"

Both men gaped in confusion. "Is that who was shooting?"

"Yes, along with an individual on a Kawasaki," Walsh replied.

Timothy swatted at Jessup. "Told you it was that dude!" He faced Dani. "We got to the hill and saw the cows strolling across the road. It's not easy to stop a vehicle with a heavy load."

"Did you know the people on the motorcycle?" Walsh asked.

"No, sir!" Timothy shook his head emphatically. "We were a ways back when a red Kawasaki flew around us."

"The passenger must've disembarked the bike and climbed onto the bales," Dani surmised.

"Like those awesome action movies!" Jessup exclaimed.

"We figured it was one of those kids with the body or helmet cams doing stunts," Timothy said.

"Did the motorcycle shooters also release the cows to trap us?" Dani asked Walsh.

"Possibly. I'll call this in," Walsh said, reaching for his phone.

Dani half-heartedly listened to Walsh as the two men spoke excitedly about the incident. "Please stay here," she said, moving closer to inspect the ground. The thick tire tread revealed the motorcycle had gone into the pasture at the break in the fence, confirming the presumption the biker had forced the cows onto the road.

Walsh approached. "State patrol is on the way. I also requested a hauler to help with the hay bale," he informed the men.

They walked with the drivers to survey the damage. Jessup took off his baseball cap and swiped at his head. "I'm really sorry about this."

"Yeah, that's not good," Timothy replied.

Sirens sounded in the distance, announcing the state troopers.

"I'll talk with NSP." Walsh turned toward the strobing lights.

"Knox and I can help with the cows," Dani offered. She glanced down. "Ready to work, Knox?"

The K-9's entire back end wagged with excitement.

She pointed to the closest animals. "Go!"

The Dobie mix darted past her, starting at the rear of the herd and yelped sharply. Irritated at the canine, a cow mooed annoyance, but with a few more probing yelps, Knox got the animal moving. The group watched in amusement as the dog herded the remaining loiterers into the pasture.

The troopers secured the gate, ensuring they didn't have a repeat escape. Dani surveyed the landscape, listening as the semi drivers spoke with the officers processing the scene.

"They appear genuine," Walsh said, sidling up next to her and nodding at Timothy and Jessup.

"Yeah, but it played out conveniently, right? The cows, the truck, the shooting," Dani said.

"You think they were working with the shooter?"

"I don't know."

"If the motorcyclist broke the fence to release and push the animals through, the rest was easy," Walsh said.

Two hours later, riding in the SUV Skyler and Graham had dropped off for them, Walsh pulled off the country road outside Humphrey. He drove up a curved lane to a ridiculously prodigious estate set amid a burbling fountain and stone pillars.

"This is Raymond Strauss's home?" Dani asked, disgust in her tone.

"Yep."

"How do you know he'll be there?"

"Eliana checked his online calendar, and it shows he's teleworking today."

"Nice," Dani replied. "Think he'll have an issue with me bringing Knox?" She jerked her chin toward the rear kennel where the dog sat.

"Knox is an officer as far as the law is concerned." Walsh shut off the engine. "He goes where we go."

She gave him an appreciative smile as they exited

the vehicle. Dani leashed Knox, and they walked up the short sidewalk to the double glass doors.

"Talk about overbuilding for a neighborhood," Dani mumbled.

"Right?" Walsh strode beside her. "Defending criminals is apparently lucrative." He knocked on the door, then pressed the doorbell and casually positioned himself in front of the camera sensor to block the view.

"You're bad." Dani chuckled.

He offered her an innocent shrug. "What?"

Several seconds ticked by without a response. Walsh rang the bell again and, finally, footsteps sounded before a voice asked, "Who is it?"

"Deputy US Marshal."

A long pause and the locks clicked. Raymond Strauss, looking as Walsh remembered, stood on the opposite side. He wore shorts and a loose-fitting, button-up shirt, clearly dressed in casual attire. "What's this about, Marshal?" The man was easily a foot shorter than Walsh and his thick dark hair still bore the shaping of a 1980s feathered cut.

"Just need a moment to talk with you about one of your clients," Walsh said.

Strauss hesitated.

Would he demand a warrant?

"We won't be long," Dani declared, holding Knox's leash. "We have a few questions."

Strauss, ever the charmer, glanced up at her. "Sure, come in." He gave Knox a double-take before stepping aside.

Walsh stifled a grin as he entered behind Dani.

"My office is straight to the back," Strauss said, closing the door.

They strolled through the elaborate main level, complete with marble floors and pillars. Strauss's office, with floor-to-ceiling cathedral windows, was at the furthest end of the building.

Walsh and Dani took opposite seats at the octagon conference table centered in the room. Both he and Dani had chosen chairs that provided them a full visual of the doorway and the windows. Knox dropped to a sit beside Dani.

"Officers, how can I help you?" Strauss meandered to the chair at the far end of the table. His light tone didn't match the perspiration already soaking the armpits of his shirt and shining on his forehead. He spoke to Dani, keeping a reasonable distance, no doubt because of Knox.

"This is my colleague, Chief Danielle Fontaine," Walsh introduced.

Dani kept her palm on Knox's head in a silent warning. Walsh surmised her body language was also an avoidance to shake Strauss's outstretched hand.

"Pleased to meet you," Strauss said, taking the hint and settling into his seat. Walsh didn't miss the effort to show dominance.

"Has Enrique Prachank contacted you recently?" Walsh asked.

Strauss leaned forward, feigning interest. "Enrique is incarcerated, awaiting trial."

The man was a horrible liar. "I'm sure you're aware

he is a fugitive who escaped custody some time ago," Walsh replied.

The attorney furrowed his brows and tapped at his temple as though in deep thought. "Oh, that's right. Sorry, I confused him with another Enrique I'm currently representing. It's a common name." He flashed a toothy grin. "I remember now. No, I haven't spoken with Mr. Prachank since his hearing. I'm certain he understands there's not much I can do for him since he's a fugitive."

Dani shot Walsh a glower. "He's not tried contacting you?"

"Officer—" Strauss began.

"Chief," Dani corrected him.

"My apologies." Strauss placed a hand to his chest in an exaggerated effort. *"Chief—"* he emphasized the word "—my job is to protect my clients to the full extent of the law. I take that responsibility seriously. Especially because law enforcement has falsely accused several." He held up both hands in surrender. "Not that you fine folks would do that."

"We need to talk with Prachank directly," Walsh added. "You're certainly welcome to be present during that questioning. However, the matter is of utmost importance."

"As I've stated, Marshal, Mr. Prachank hasn't contacted me," Strauss said coolly. "I am curious what this is in regard to?"

"An ongoing investigation that includes attempted murder charges," Dani replied.

"Prachank was already charged with multiple

counts of homicide," Strauss explained. "All of which were loosely tied to him by a single weapon. When we have our day in court, we'll disprove that accusation."

"Or it will seal his fate." Walsh gritted his teeth. Was the man serious? "He puts illegal weapons on the streets for criminals to use. He's most definitely no law-abiding citizen."

"Let's save our arguments for the courtroom, Marshal." Strauss exhaled. "Again, I haven't heard from him. But should that change, I'll be in touch with you both at the earliest possible convenience."

Clearly, Strauss was attempting to dismiss them, but Walsh refused to give up. "There's been a recent development in Prachank's case. Should he contact you, there might be an opportunity for him to contribute to the investigation." He paused for effect. "I'm sure I don't need to remind you how cooperation could bode well for him with the authorities."

Strauss opened his mouth, then closed it again.

Walsh pushed away from the table, and Dani mimicked him.

"Thank you for your time." She slid a business card toward the attorney.

Together they exited the house, not speaking until they were inside the safety of the SUV.

"Is he telling the truth?" Dani asked, snapping on her seat belt.

"That's debatable, but based on his responses, he's not communicating with Prachank." Walsh donned his sunglasses. "If he has, maybe the lure of a deal will bring the fugitive out from under his slimy hidey-hole."

"Now where to?" Dani asked.

"The Rock to touch base with the team. I'm hoping they'll have an update for us."

"First, let me check on Jayne," Dani said, withdrawing her phone.

Walsh listened in on the call. By her downcast expression and tone inflection, he surmised it wasn't good news. When she disconnected, he asked, "Any change?"

"None. She's still in critical condition and hasn't regained consciousness." Dani leaned back in her seat with a sigh. "How did I get here?"

"Over the past few years, I've asked that question a lot," Walsh confessed.

Dani faced him. "Tell me about Prachank's case. I'm only familiar with the media's reports."

"He's a skilled manipulator and has outstanding sales skills. He also has connections deep in militia groups and cartels. We worked hard to bring him down. Getting his last cache of weapons was a monumental victory. Solid evidence against him. A pistol registered to him—"

"Wait, let me get this straight. He legally owned a gun?"

"On paper, but we discovered he was running weapons in an underground trafficking effort. We tied the one pistol registered to him to the triple homicide."

"That's the missing gun?" Dani asked.

"Yes. We didn't have strong enough evidence against him for arms trafficking, but the murder charges carry more time behind bars. We want to ensure Prachank isn't on the streets anymore."

"Strauss said there was only a loose connection to Prachank."

Walsh snorted. "That's been their defense from the start. Prachank claimed someone stole the gun before the murders, and it happened to appear at his home prior to the takedown. He insisted the same person planted it there to frame him."

"Prachank stuck around Nebraska and stole his weapon only to use it on us? That's ridiculous."

"I agree. A lot of this is bizarre." Walsh inhaled. "Except the connective dots lead to Jayne. She had access. Whether she gave it to Prachank willingly or under coercion is the bigger question."

"She wouldn't do that," Dani argued. Her jaw set tight and stubborn.

"I understand you care about her, like you did Chief Varmose."

Anger flashed in Dani's blue eyes, and she averted her gaze. "Don't bring up ancient history. It's not helpful."

Walsh considered the words, disagreeing. He remained silent.

Just as she'd initially refused to acknowledge the corrupt practices of her old chief, she was unwilling to see the obvious signs in front of her face. He had to prove Jayne's involvement, and that would come when he uncovered the connection between the evidence technician and Prachank. And he needed to do it before anyone else got hurt.

# FIVE

Dani fought the urge to defend herself in another battle with Walsh. How dare he bring up their painful past.

Recollections of the incident with Varmose returned. She'd trusted her then boyfriend, Beckham Walsh, who had gone behind her back, secretly collecting evidence against her chief. His investigation had set her up with the other Cortez PD officers. Of course, they'd believed she was in on the takedown and that she'd worked with Walsh to gain Varmose's trust. Surely, Walsh remembered that little detail.

He had unfairly blindsided her by arresting Varmose. She had caught the aftermath of the investigation, bearing the disdain of the other officers until she'd surrendered and transferred to a different station to escape the hatred. If Walsh wasn't aware of that, she'd not give him the satisfaction of sharing her pain. Especially not when he was throwing her naïveté in her face again.

"I'm just saying…" Walsh interrupted her thoughts. "You're too close to the problem."

Unable to hold her tongue any longer, she blurted, "I was wrong about Varmose then, but that's not the situation with Jayne."

Walsh glanced at her. "Dani, I'm not blaming you. We must remain objective."

Right. Like she believed that. "I am, and that includes consideration of the verifiable facts that I can provide. Jayne has proved herself trustworthy over the years."

He sighed, clearly annoyed with her, and despite her brain's demand to stop defending Jayne, Dani added, "I was young and trusted my commander. You can't hold that against me."

"Varmose's behavior is totally on him."

"But you think I'm naïve, like I was back then, and I don't see the truth about Jayne. This isn't the same scenario."

"Whoa. First, I never said you were naïve. Second, if you're unwilling to be honest about Jayne's involvement, either with yourself or my team, recuse yourself from this investigation."

Dani opened her mouth to defend her position, but Walsh went on. "If that's not an issue, then don't worry about it." Something in his tone told Dani that he'd made up his mind.

Frustrated, she turned away, and they rode in silence to the HFTF headquarters. Recusing herself wasn't an option. Jayne needed an advocate. Dani owed her that. She hoped to remain unbiased, but the weight of Tessa's future, and Jayne's life, hung heavy on her. Separating her emotions from the case evidence was a difficult but not impossible request.

The team had assembled in the Rock, actively working as Dani and Walsh entered. While he addressed them, Dani moved to check on Tessa where she slept peacefully in the Pack 'n Play near Eliana.

"She's a sweetheart," Eliana said, rolling to face Dani.

Dani slid into the chair beside her. "Thank you for babysitting. I realize this can't happen regularly."

Eliana tilted her head, compassion written in her expression. "It's hard to see an innocent child caught in the middle of such a difficult situation."

Emotion tightened Dani's throat. "Exactly." She leaned over Tessa, restraining the urge to stroke the infant's feathery-soft hair.

The room filled with chatter and discussion pertinent to the case, and Dani listened as the group bounced ideas and details off one another.

"People, assemble and update," Walsh commanded.

Dani marveled at how the task force cooperated effortlessly, like a perfectly oiled law enforcement machine. They sat around the table, joining Dani and Eliana, with Walsh at the head, furthest from Dani. As usual.

Was she reading too much into his actions, or was he deliberately keeping his distance from her?

"Skyler, any word from NIBIN?" Walsh asked.

"*Sí.*" She scooted closer, holding a folder. "We dug into all the inventory that our team had logged at GIPD, and discovered there were several weapons stolen from other cases."

Walsh leaned forward. "Besides the Prachank case?"

"Yes," Tiandra replied.

Dani gaped. "How?"

"That is the ultimate question," Riker said.

"Our most worrisome is the compromised illegal munitions we seized four years ago," Skyler said.

"The militia investigation?" Eliana clarified.

"Yep." Skyler shook her head. "That was significant firepower that has no place on the streets."

"As in military-grade artillery?" Dani asked. The group remained quiet, answering with their silence.

"It was one of our first cases," Tiandra explained. "We seized it all from a mountain militia in South Dakota."

Dani studied each member, feeling the weight of their scrutinizing stares on her. This was more than a few missing pieces of evidence. Not that it wasn't significant, but military munitions raised the stakes. "How did this happen?" Dani whispered.

"Are there specific arms that create a pattern or are they random items?" Walsh asked.

"Random, as far as we can tell," Chance said.

"Tiandra, Elijah and I will conduct a thorough inventory at the GIPD offices," Graham advised. "We'll know more once that's completed."

"Did someone send their grocery list of weapons and have Jayne steal them?" Walsh asked.

Dani glared at him. "There's no proof Jayne's responsible." Even as she spoke the defense, she doubted herself.

"That's a viable possibility," Graham replied.

"Identifying who stole the artillery and/or who ordered them is crucial," Tiandra added.

"Yes," Elijah responded, touching her hand.

Dani did a double-take. They were together too?

Tiandra's cheeks blushed a rosy hue. "Elijah and I are engaged."

Dani blinked. "So, Riker and Eliana." She pointed to the couple, then shifted, pointing at Tiandra. "And you and Elijah?"

"It's bonkers, right?" Skyler rolled her eyes.

"Wow." Dani's mind reeled with the information. Here they were, personally connected, while Walsh raked her over the coals for her and Jayne's friendship. She'd deal with him in private.

As though reading her thoughts, Skyler said, "Dani knows Jayne best. She's our closest connection to Jayne and offers that personal insight we won't gain by digging through evidence."

Gratitude for the comment softened Dani's bitter viewpoint and reminded her that without HFTF conducting the inventory, another agency would perform an internal affairs investigation on her department. That would openly expose the incompetency, and Jayne might face criminal charges based on the circumstantial evidence. Not to mention, Dani being recused from her position as chief. She glanced at Walsh. Her life and that of her friend depended on a man she'd never fully trust. Yet, where else did she have to go?

They were letting her contribute to the case. She had to stop defending Jayne and find proof to exonerate her.

"Dani, would Jayne have any reason to betray you?" Tiandra asked.

Defensiveness raged through Dani, but she fought

the urge to lash out at the FBI agent who'd posed a valid question. "None that I can think of. For her to do so jeopardizes her career and custody of her child. Why would she take such enormous risks?"

"You said the baby's father is deceased?" Eliana asked.

"Yes." Dani sighed.

Tessa grunted and rolled over, facing Dani. She rose to gather a bottle just as the baby erupted into loud wails. Dani hurried to prepare the formula, quickly appeasing the infant. Though the team made no protests to having her there, she caught Walsh's gaze. They weren't a babysitting service. She had to find care for Tessa if she had any hope of clearing Jayne's name before an outside agency took over the investigation.

Dani inhaled a fortifying breath and sat with Tessa in her arms while she greedily devoured the bottle. The team's attention rotated to the evidence board already in progress. They'd linked pictures of the criminals and weapons from their prior cases with red lines. Interestingly, none of them intersected.

Tessa finished, and Dani repositioned the infant to burp her. She cooed contentedly over Dani's shoulder. "Is it possible the stolen artillery isn't about Jayne at all? The common denominator is HFTF."

As though she'd revealed a huge epiphany, the team faced the evidence board.

"She's correct," Tiandra agreed.

"Beyond the compromised GIPD evidence locker

location, all were linked to cases you worked," Dani said, confidence building.

"Can't disagree," Graham replied. "Great job, Dani."

"I'll make some calls. You all keep working," Walsh said, and the group stood for dismissal.

"Elijah and I will head back to the evidence locker," Graham said.

"I could go with you," Dani replied, gazing down at Tessa. How was she supposed to care for the baby and work simultaneously?

"Actually, with all due respect..." Graham shot a look at Walsh. Dani glanced between the men.

"Walsh hates that phrase," Elijah chuckled.

"Hmm. Well, it annoys me when he answers the phone without so much as a 'hello' before he launches into a discussion," Dani teased.

Stifled chuckles confirmed their agreement.

"Are you finished?" Walsh grunted.

"Anyway, Dani," Graham cut in, "it might be better if you're not there."

"Right." She nodded. "Keeps the investigation unbiased."

"Exactly," Elijah concluded.

Thankful they'd given her the out, Dani said, "Holler if you need anything."

"Roger that," the twins replied in unison.

"Eliana, track down the criminals, besides Prachank, linked to the missing weapons," Walsh ordered.

Dani gazed into Tessa's sweet face. Parting with

the baby broke her heart, but the best way to care for her was to help exonerate Jayne. For that, she needed to focus on the case.

The group dispersed. Resolved, Dani carried Tessa and followed Walsh to his office. She dropped into a seat opposite him.

He slid into his desk chair and faced her. "You have something on your mind."

"You're right. I need to devote my attention to the case, and I can't do that while providing the care that Tessa needs." Her mother had spent her life demonstrating the impossible task, which had solidified Dani's notions that marriage and family didn't mix with work. "My devotion is to uphold the law to the best of my abilities. That must come first."

Walsh leaned back in his seat. Dani expected to see satisfaction in his expression. Instead, he said, "I can't imagine the difficulty you're facing. Torn between keeping Tessa safe with you and handing her over to Child Protective Services is no simple choice."

His compassion nearly undid her. She could deal with their contentious relationship, but Walsh's gentle and understanding tone proved more difficult. Dani's heart recalled the reasons she'd first fallen for him. His kindness and the way she felt safe with him combined with his rugged handsomeness. Her gaze traveled the contours of his face. Remembering his touch and their shared tender kisses. Dani looked down. *Get a hold of yourself.* "I've never had the responsibility for a child before."

Walsh nodded.

"One request." Dani met his gaze. "I have to meet the person caring for her first."

"That's totally reasonable. Would you like me to make the call and set things up?"

"Yes, please."

Walsh lifted the receiver of his desk phone.

Tessa squirmed, and Dani got to her feet, slipping out of his office.

Was it a betrayal to Jayne if Dani wasn't the one personally providing Tessa's care? Caught between an impassable mountain and a wall of fire, Dani didn't know which was worse.

By the time Walsh and Dani had evaluated the foster home options available for Tessa, the sun was fading on the horizon. They pulled up to the large ranch-style house set on an acreage north of Lincoln in Valparaiso.

"Such a beautiful property," Dani whispered. "Not what I pictured."

"Me either," Walsh replied.

The expansive house stretched out with the double front door centering the structure. A four-car attached garage to the left side permitted them space to park in the driveway.

Children's outdoor toys were scattered around the pristine lawn. Flowers in a variety of bright colors created a boundary along the sidewalk. Perfectly trimmed bushes lined the white banister rails of the wraparound front porch. A picturesque scene.

Walsh shut off the engine, and Dani threw open her

door wordlessly. Was she second-guessing her decision to leave Tessa with the foster family?

They'd left Knox at the Rock, unsure how the transition would go. Now Walsh wondered if that had been a mistake. The dog would no doubt offer Dani the emotional support she'd need to do this.

Dani released Tessa's carrier and the base from the backseat, and he followed her to the sidewalk and up the front porch steps. The aroma of something delicious wafted to them from the open windows. Walsh's stomach grumbled, and he realized they'd not taken the time to eat that day. Dani shot him a confused look, and his neck warmed. "Guess missing breakfast and lunch wasn't a great idea," he confessed, rapping softly on the door.

"I haven't had an appetite since this all started." Dani turned to face him. "I feel like I'm abandoning her."

"You're not," Walsh assured her. Then he posed the question he didn't want to hear the answer to. "Are you having doubts about leaving her here?"

"Can't say until after we've sat and talked to them. If I don't have any red flags as far as the house or their behavior, then no regrets. Otherwise, I may change my mind and take her with us."

"My contact, Mrs. Terrote, at CPS confided she highly recommends them and calls the Ibarras her best family," he said. Walsh didn't add that he'd requested the most trustworthy vetted parents CPS had on file. Mrs. Terrote hadn't taken the request lightly, knowing Walsh wouldn't make an appeal flippantly.

Footsteps drew closer, and they stepped back as the front door opened. A thirtysomething woman dressed in athletic shorts and a T-shirt with flowery letters that read Ask Me About My Kids, smiled at them. She'd pulled her auburn hair into a loose ponytail, and she wore no makeup.

"Mrs. Ibarra?" Walsh asked, since Dani seemed unable to speak.

"Sadie, please." She extended a hand. "You must be Chief Fontaine and Commander Walsh."

"Call me Dani." She shook Sadie's hand, regaining her professional composure. "Yes, thank you for seeing us on such short notice."

"Beckham," Walsh said.

Sadie stepped aside, waving them in. "Perry is putting down the kids. He'll join us in a few minutes."

They entered the spacious living room where a massive U-shaped couch centered the space. Shelves with children's toys neatly filled one side, and nothing appeared out of place.

"Have a seat." Sadie dropped onto the sofa.

Dani and Walsh took seats at the opposite end. "And this must be sweet Tessa." Sadie leaned with her elbows on her knees, smiling at the baby.

Dani shifted Tessa to sit facing forward. The infant held on to Dani's fingers and cooed happily. "How many children do you have?"

"Depends on the day. We offer emergency care, so sometimes we have little ones with us for a few days before CPS places them in permanent housing,"

Sadie explained. "Currently, we have four. Ages eighteen months, six years old, and eight-year-old twins."

Dani nodded, and a frown crossed her face. "Will you have time for Tessa without compromising on the care of the other children?"

Sadie appeared nonplussed by the direct question. "Absolutely. She'll have all the attention and love possible while she's with us. Perry telecommutes, providing him the availability to help with the children's daily needs."

"One of the significant advantages of working from home," a tall, lanky man added, entering the room. He sported a spiky haircut with his shock of red hair. "Sorry for the delay. I'm Perry." He extended a hand, addressing Walsh before moving to Dani.

"We try to keep their lives as normal as possible," Sadie said as her husband sat beside her.

He smiled kindly. "We've fostered children from many types of situations," he replied. "The goal is to reunite them as long as it's in the best interest of the child."

"Good," Dani said, lifting her chin. "Just to be clear, as soon as Jayne's recovered, they'll be reunited."

"Mrs. Terrote from CPS filled us in a bit on the situation," Sadie said. "We're praying for Ms. Bardot's total recovery."

Dani interrogated the couple, and Walsh listened, feeling like an intruder to a personal conversation. She withheld nothing, pointedly making her queries. But he understood she needed reassurance that Tessa was in the best possible care. Her posture softened slightly, and the Ibarras seemed nonplussed by the inquisition.

They offered a tour of the home, which appeared clean and welcoming. Children's drawings plastered the large refrigerator in the kitchen. And Sadie showed them the room where Tessa would stay before they peeked in on the other sleeping children.

When they returned to the main floor, Dani still cuddled Tessa close, rubbing the baby's back with one hand. "I'll try to visit as often as possible until Jayne recovers," she pledged. She gingerly passed Tessa to Sadie, and the baby giggled as the woman tickled her arm and spoke in a soft voice.

"Thank you again, and please don't hesitate to contact either of us if you have any concerns or questions," Walsh said, handing Perry his business card.

"I'll call for daily updates," Dani said.

"Absolutely," Sadie replied, and Tessa turned, smiling at Dani as though reassuring her everything would be all right.

Walsh moved toward the door, and Dani stayed close beside him. They exited the house after another rendition of goodbyes and walked to the SUV. The wind had picked up in heavy gusts.

After they'd both climbed inside the vehicle, Dani said, "I hate this."

"I know." Walsh inserted his key and turned it to start the engine. The car dinged with a message light warning the trunk was open. "That's weird."

"What's wrong?" Dani leaned closer.

Walsh thought back. Had they put any of Tessa's things in the trunk? He didn't recall opening it and removing items before walking into the Ibarras' home.

The hairs on his arms rose in a visceral response. He scanned the surroundings, but night had settled.

"Dani, get out of the vehicle. Now!" He kept his tone calm and firm.

"Why?" Her eyes widened as she threw open her door simultaneously with him.

They leapt from the SUV, scurrying as far as possible and taking shelter near the house.

Several long seconds passed.

Images of his tours in the Middle East where IEDs exploded his unit's military vehicles, and the desperate shouts of innocent civilians invaded his mind. Walsh shook off the painful memories. Had he overreacted, transferring his past into the present?

Dani quirked a brow at him.

"Guess I—"

An explosion rocked the ground, and the SUV went up in flames.

# SIX

Dani stepped back, gasping for breath.

Night had descended, which enhanced the orange-and-red blaze that devoured Walsh's SUV. The flames danced with the increasingly strong wind, stretching high into the sky. A gust whistled eerily through the trees, and toys skipped across the yard.

Dani turned to Walsh. "What just—"

A loud pop sent them diving to the ground. They scurried for cover, hiding on the side of the porch. Shots pinged around them, impaling the railing. They scoured the inky landscape for the shooter's location.

Together, she and Walsh hurried up the steps, pelted by chips of spraying wood from the rapid gunfire. "It's coming from the tree line," Walsh advised.

From their protected positions, they returned fire in the direction of the shooter.

Dani briefly twisted to look at the windows of the Ibarra home behind her. "We have to warn them!" She prayed the Ibarras wouldn't open the door at the wrong time.

At last, the shooting ceased.

The air became too still, thrusting Dani and Walsh into a creepy silence.

They surveyed the area, unsure where the shooter had gone or if he continued to watch them. The vast copse of trees offered their assailant many places to hide while they remained exposed on the front porch.

When several seconds passed without further incident, Dani beat on the door. "Mr. Ibarra! Let us in!"

Walsh hollered into his cell phone for backup and rescue personnel.

Crouched low, Dani prepared to tackle whoever answered. At last, the door cracked open, and she met Sadie—also in a squatted position.

"We heard the gunshots."

Dani and Walsh scurried inside, closing the door behind them.

"Was anyone hurt?" Dani asked.

"No," Sadie said, no quiver in her voice. "Everyone is safe."

"I've contacted rescue and fire personnel." Walsh stepped up to the windows, tugging the blinds and curtains closed. "Keep the lights off. We don't want to give away our location to the shooter."

Perry and Sadie stayed clear of the entrance. She held Tessa.

"Did someone blow up your vehicle?" Perry asked.

"Yes," Walsh replied.

"Get the children," Dani ordered, rushing toward them.

As though snapping to the present, Perry made eye contact with her before he spun on his heel and scurried down the hallway.

"Please give me Tessa," Dani said, reaching for the baby.

Sadie didn't argue, gently passing the infant to her. "What just happened?"

Dani considered her next words. She didn't want to

frighten the Ibarras, however, she had to convey the severity of the situation. "Gather the children. Grab any essentials, prescriptions, et cetera, and meet us back here ASAP!"

"Steer clear of the windows and stay low," Walsh added.

Sadie nodded and turned, following her husband down the hallway to the bedrooms.

Walsh glanced out a corner of the curtains. "I think the shooter fled."

"Could you estimate the gunman's position?"

"No. He was a lousy shot or it wasn't a scoped rifle," Walsh said. "Thankfully, he missed. A lot."

"Yeah. The wind certainly helped," Dani added.

Once they'd gathered Tessa's belongings, they sat in the dining room shielded by the interior walls.

"Are the Ibarras in danger after we leave?" Dani whispered, holding Tessa close to her chest.

"I hope not, but let's not take any chances. They need to find a place to stay tonight. I'll have the team sweep the house before they return."

The familiar shriek of sirens promised assistance.

"How did someone get a bomb into your SUV?"

"It was unattended while we were inside." Walsh shook his head. "I should've stayed outside on guard."

"I can't believe this." Dani shivered. She ducked low and peered out the corner of the dining room curtain. The land stretched far into the expansive darkness, leaving her feeling vulnerable. "Is he still watching us?"

Never one to mince words, Walsh stated the obvious. "It's possible, but with responders on the way, I don't think he'll shoot at us again."

"I'd be surprised if he set the bomb and left."

"Agreed."

"But why here?"

Walsh leaned back in the chair. "Nobody but my contact at CPS was aware we were coming to the Ibarras'."

"Is that person involved?"

"Doubtful," Walsh said. "My guess is he followed us here."

"None of your acquaintances have the propensity to be corrupt?" The comment was out of line, and Dani bit her lip. "Sorry, that was uncalled for."

"We won't rule anybody out until we have evidence to support it," Walsh assured her.

"What if he put the bomb in the SUV at the Rock?"

"Negative. There are too many surveillance cameras there," Walsh's tone was unconvincing.

"Why not attack us on the road? Why wait until we're here with Tessa?" Even as she spoke, the thought assailed her. "Unless…am I in danger or is Tessa?"

Walsh studied her. "I want to believe nobody is malicious enough to target an innocent baby, but unfortunately, it's not out of the realm of possibility."

How could she leave Tessa if she was in danger? But if the threat was to Dani, how could she keep Tessa close?

Rescue personnel pulled onto the property, and Walsh took the escape, hurrying out the door to greet them. Dani got to her feet and walked into the Ibarras' bedroom. "It's safe for us to go now."

Sadie held a frail toddler in her arms. Perry carried a six-year-old on his hip while he gently ushered twin girls from the room.

In a mute march, the group exited the house and paused. Destruction from the bullets scarred the beautiful wraparound porch. Sadie appeared to take in the damage and her lip quivered, but she said nothing.

"Please wait here. I'll find out what the next steps are," Dani said.

She hurried to Walsh, who stood beside a Valparaiso police cruiser.

Firefighters worked to extinguish the flames, and the strobing lights filled the night sky.

Dani paused at a distance, not wanting to interrupt Walsh's conversation. "I'd appreciate that," he said to the officer before turning and walking to her.

A chill snaked up her spine with the sensation that the bomber was watching them. Surely, he'd wonder if he'd completed his task.

"Let's have the kids move toward the fire engines," Walsh said. "It'll lessen their fear if we make it fun."

"Okay." She glanced over her shoulder to where the Ibarras sat on the porch.

Perry held the toddler on his lap, and the child rubbed his eyes.

Sadie draped her arms protectively over the six-year-old girl and the twins.

"Hey, guys, I'm Commander Walsh." He approached slowly, his tone light. "Have you ever seen a fire engine up close before?"

The twins shook their heads in synchronicity and the six-year-old sucked her thumb.

"Great! Let me show you." Walsh tenderly led the group down the stairs. "This is my friend, Dani. She's going to walk over with you, so baby Tessa can also see the truck."

Dani took her cue and plastered a smile on her face. "Come on." She waved with one hand.

Sadie gave her a confused look, then seemed to understand and joined the discussion. "We don't get many chances to do this. What an adventure."

The group moved toward the largest rig, where firefighters unrolled hoses and shouted orders. Two paramedics stepped out of the ambulance. Parked behind the fire truck sat an SUV with Battalion Chief printed across the side. Walsh offered a wave to the man climbing out of the SUV. He wore a white uniform shirt and dark pants. Based on the way he smiled at them, Dani assumed Walsh must've already told him about the situation.

"Let's start with stickers!" the chief said, passing out small plastic badges with the fire department emblem printed on them.

The kids cautiously approached him, their apprehension slowly lessening in the officer's presence. He chatted easily with them, even getting a couple of grins. He rattled off the names of the equipment and engaged the children in the discussion.

The adults stayed back, giving him room.

"Thank you," Sadie whispered.

"You all will need to find some place to stay tonight," Walsh said, joining the conversation. "My team is on the way, and they'll ensure there are no additional detonation devices, but it would be best to keep the kids away for the night."

Perry stepped closer, slowly lowering the wriggling toddler to the ground. The baby waddled toward the fire chief and the other children. "Not a problem," Perry said, glancing over his shoulder.

Sadie nodded. "We have family not far from here. We'll stay with them."

"I'm sorry," Dani said. How had she not considered the horrific possibility that the attacker might come after them here?

The fire chief reached into his vehicle and handed the kids tattoos and plastic fire hats, eliciting cheers.

Dani smiled at his efforts.

"Do you need any help collecting supplies before you go?" Walsh asked.

"No, we're ready," Sadie replied.

Two black SUVs drove up on the property. "That's my team," Walsh said. "I'll be right back."

Sadie reached out and patted Tessa's back. "She's a sweet baby. I know you'll take good care of her."

Dani glanced up, meeting Sadie's soft brown eyes. Words eluded her. She'd never cared for another human being, certainly not one this tiny. She wanted to tell Sadie that standing here with Tessa she felt more inadequate than ever.

Sadie squeezed her shoulder, then hurried to meet Perry and corral the children.

Walsh approached with Tiandra, K-9 Bosco, and

Skyler trailing. Dani spun to face them, and they stood at a distance from the SUV, which sat in a dripping mess from the fire extinguishers.

"Tiandra and Bosco will search the Ibarras' house for any other explosives," Walsh explained.

"We'll maintain perimeter watch and conduct evidence collection," Skyler said.

"Meet at the Rock at 0800. If you're still working the scene here, connect via video conference once we're there," Walsh said.

"Thank you," Dani replied.

She longed to say more, but the current situation overwhelmed her. The bomber's motive and intentions had endangered too many lives. If the target was on her or Tessa, they had to be wiser.

The garage door opened, revealing Perry and Sadie as they loaded the children into a large minivan. Any of them could've died in the gunfire and explosion. Her stomach roiled. How far would this person go to kill her? Tessa cooed, and she looked down at the baby. Or was Tessa his target, and if so, why?

The next morning, Walsh leaned back in his office chair, still exhausted from days of no sleep. The team would arrive soon, and he had no clue where to steer the investigation.

He spotted Dani and Tessa in the conference room, where the glass wall offered him a clear view. They needed a better solution for Tessa's care. Whoever had targeted Dani and/or Tessa was relentless. Only his team could handle their protective detail. It was too risky to put the infant in a foster home.

Or perhaps that was his own bias. He had to protect them.

For a single moment, Walsh allowed his mind to consider what it would've been like to father his own child. Now that retirement hovered like a vulture waiting to consume its prey, those dreams had faded into the impossible. But in the years when life was good with Gwen, and they'd talked about having a family of their own, he'd dared to hope.

He glanced down at his desk and lifted the expensive Montblanc pen Gwen had given him for their first Christmas. Why he kept it, Walsh couldn't explain. It didn't even write anymore. He'd eliminated all other remnants of her memory from his home and office, but the Montblanc pen always accompanied him. It also reminded him of his failures to protect Gwen and to be there when she'd needed him most. It served as a penance for his selfishness that had cost Gwen's life and their future together.

Yet, spending time with Dani had awakened his heart again, resuscitating his dreams and the feelings he'd buried for Dani even before Gwen came into his life. Prior to the Varmose case, he'd felt certain he'd marry Dani. They'd shared the most wonderful romance. A vulnerability he'd never known consumed Walsh. The swirling emotions made him wonder if God would give him a second chance to love.

No. He'd failed Gwen, and now he was doing the same with Tessa and Dani. Walsh shook off the thoughts. He didn't deserve happiness. Gwen's parents had reminded him of that unmercifully, reinforcing his personal vow to remain a bachelor. *A man needs to protect his wife.* He hadn't done that. Gwen's father's accusations replayed in his mind.

How was it possible that he'd come full circle again? Frustration as his ineptitude to safeguard Dani and Tessa, not to mention the entire Ibarra family weighed on Walsh. Perhaps it was time he retired.

No. Not until he finished this case.

He would get his head in the game and find the bomber/shooter.

Renewed by his mission, Walsh stood and snagged his files off the desk. He exited his office just as Skyler and Tiandra entered the Rock with K-9 Bosco, Elijah, and Graham behind them.

Riker, K-9 Ammo, and Eliana trailed with Chance and K-9 Destiny. The team had arrived, and it was time to get to work. Chance carried a long flat box of what Walsh hoped held breakfast.

He joined the group as everyone settled around the table. Chance slid the box into the center.

"Thanks," Eliana said, passing out napkins.

"He's still trying to earn favor," Elijah teased.

"Just for that, you don't get any." Tiandra swatted playfully at her fiancé, and he leaned over, kissing her forehead.

Walsh's heart swelled for his team—no, his family. As he encroached to the mandatory retirement age of 57, driving him from his career, Walsh's purpose for living would vanish too. What was he without his title?

Being a commander was his entire identity. What would he do when they stripped him of it in a few years?

"May I?" Graham approached Dani and reached for Tessa.

"Sure?" Her reply came out as more of a question than a statement. She passed the child to him, but her tentative gaze remained on Tessa.

Graham, being the self-absorbed and completely confident man he was, didn't appear to notice or care. He dropped onto the seat, sitting the infant on the tabletop in front of him. He cooed and made silly faces, gaining baby giggles.

Walsh gawked. "How did we not know this about you, Graham?"

"Is that not normal behavior for him?" Dani asked.

"Of course it is," Skyler teased. "He's a charmer."

"No, the accident softened him," Tiandra said.

"You're all wrong," Graham replied, glancing over Tessa's head. "I have always had a gift for communicating with babies. Ask Elijah."

Elijah sat with a donut stuffed in his mouth and shrugged.

"All right, settle in and recap where we are." Walsh surveyed his team.

God had brought him an incredible group of skilled and capable people. He considered himself blessed to work with them. A twinge of sadness lingered as he debated how soon that would end. Exactly why he was developing his successor.

"Skyler, take the lead." He'd already begun working with the talented AFT agent, prepared to pass down the title of commander to her when the time came. Though he'd not shared that with her yet.

"Tiandra and I—" Bosco sidled up to Skyler with a whine. "My apologies. *Bosco*, Tiandra, and I," she corrected, earning a hearty laugh from the team, "conducted the surveillance and perimeter search. We found no other explosives on the property and released the house to the Ibarras first thing this morning."

"The assailant placed the bomb at the rear of your SUV," Tiandra added. "It appears he failed to notice the strap that interfered with the trunk lid closing completely. That's what saved your lives."

"He followed us there and then put the explosive inside?" Dani asked.

"I locked the vehicle," Walsh said, then second-guessed himself.

"It's easy enough to break into with an electronic decoder," Graham said, never taking his eyes off Tessa's head before resuming his baby talk and silly faces.

"Is your brother all right?" Tiandra whispered to Elijah.

He chuckled, biting into another chocolate-frosted donut. "Yeah, he's a sucker for babies."

"Was that attack intended for Dani or Tessa?" Skyler asked.

"Or both," Chance added.

"But why Tessa? She's an innocent," Dani interjected.

"That's an important clue for us to unravel," Skyler replied. "If Tessa is a threat to the attacker, was she the planned target instead of Jayne?"

"Surely all this goes toward proving Jayne's innocence, too," Dani said.

"It definitely moves in her favor," Walsh agreed. "I think it's safe to deduce Jayne had essential information that the assailant wants. Her relationship or connection to that person is key."

Chance tilted his head, studying the evidence board. "What threat is an innocent baby to the bomber?"

They all glanced at Tessa, still enthralled with Graham's silly antics to entertain the infant.

Dani picked at a donut. "Unless the shooter was using Tessa as a way to control Jayne. Threatening to hurt her?"

"Unfortunately, that adds up," Eliana agreed. "I'd do anything to protect my child."

"If that's the case, then the assailant knows Jayne is still alive." Walsh grabbed a second donut. "I've got 24/7 protection detail on her." He considered whether that maneuver was sufficient.

"I'll also connect to the hospital's live feed and monitor through the security cameras," Eliana added.

"I need to call for an update," Dani said. "Wait, maybe I should go see her instead?"

"Negative," Walsh replied, already dialing. "I'll request they move Jayne under an assumed name to another room for now." Then to the team, "Take five while we get this handled."

Walsh called Jim Bonn, a Nebraska State Patrol captain assigned to Omaha and a close friend. When Bonn answered, Walsh blurted, "Need a favor."

"Someday, try starting conversations with 'hello,'" Bonn teased.

Walsh chuckled. "Sorry. I keep hearing that." After explaining the situation, Bonn assured he'd handle the request.

They disconnected, and Walsh returned to the table. Dani sat, posture deflated.

"I take it there's no change in Jayne's status?"

"Her condition has worsened. The next twenty-four hours are crucial."

The group stilled for a moment, weighing the seriousness of the news.

Walsh desperately fought against the urge to comfort Dani and to reassure her that everything would be fine. He couldn't do that. Not from a command position standpoint, since he wasn't sure what would happen to Jayne. Her injuries were serious.

Conversely, from a personal view, getting that close to Dani wasn't an option for him. He'd succeeded in his career by maintaining a clear and professional distance from all women. Dani was no different. They were co-workers on a case. Nothing more, regardless of their past or the way she'd chipped at his heart's defenses. His gaze flitted to Tessa, smiling at Graham, and patting him on the head with giggles. He swallowed hard. This precious child who had nearly died on his watch.

Dani glanced over at him with a look of desperation and pain. It practically undid him.

Walsh got to his feet. "I need to make some calls," he said, excusing himself. He needed distance from Dani before he did something stupid.

# SEVEN

Two days without leads and no further attacks had stalled the team's progress until Skyler announced, "We've got an update!"

The Rock buzzed with excitement as they assembled to hear Skyler's report. Dani stood, rocking Tessa. Again, Walsh positioned himself on the furthest side of the room, away from her. Could he make his avoidance any more obvious if he tried?

"The casings we found near the edge of the Ibarras' property came back as a match in NIBIN for a shooting five years ago," Skyler said. "And it was from a gun we'd logged into a cache from one of our cases."

"A pending investigation?" Chance asked.

Skyler shook her head. "No. Closed and marked for destruction."

"What?" Eliana's confusion was obvious. "I thought we kept evidence forever."

"After the case is closed, they're sent to a munitions destruction contractor," Tiandra clarified.

That was news to Dani, but she remained quiet and listened.

"Fantastic. Our criminal is taking old and new weapons?" Chance exhaled. "Why not steal those marked for destruction? We'd have never noticed."

"Until they used the guns on the street again," Elijah put in.

"Exactly." Riker rose and wrote the notes on the evidence board.

"That seems really strange," Graham murmured.

"Yeah, his motive is evolving, or we've overlooked something," Riker agreed.

"Worse, it shows we have a serious leak in the entire system," Walsh said. "Were those weapons initially housed at GIPD?"

Dani glared. Why was he determined to make her department the scapegoat for this?

"Yes," Skyler said.

Dani stifled the groan. Jayne and HFTF remained common denominators in the case. "The weapons destruction contractor is also a viable suspect."

"He has means and opportunity." Riker updated the evidence board. "Instead of eliminating suspects, we're adding to our list."

"But we have no solid motive for any of them," Walsh added.

Grateful that Walsh considered Jayne's lack of motive, Dani said, "Unfortunately, greed is always a viable reason. Maybe the consultant was manipulating the system?"

"It's feasible," Eliana said.

"I've never heard of this person," Dani said. "Jayne didn't mention him either."

The implications were increasingly serious and getting the munitions back remained a huge priority. And her department was on the line while the evidence mounted against Jayne. For the first time, doubt about her friend's involvement crept into her mind. How would Dani prove Jayne's innocence with what they'd discovered? Was that even possible? She glanced down at sleeping Tessa and crossed the room, transferring the infant to the playpen.

The group's discussion continued while Dani fought to shove aside her personal bias and shift into investigator mode. Nothing would help Jayne or Tessa if she got stuck in the loop of useless worry and fear while trying to prove Jayne's innocence.

"Where was the cache sent for destruction?" Dani inserted her question into the conversation. "Since that's before my appointment to GI, I'm not sure."

Eliana typed away on her computer. "I'll find it."

"Chief, if you trust us to babysit Tessa, my wife, Ayla, has offered her time for a short while," Chance said. "She's on a break from her office." A buzzing interrupted him, and he glanced down at his cell phone. "Speaking of, she's here."

Dani paused midstride.

"We didn't mean to overstep, just figured you had a lot to deal with," Riker explained.

"I appreciate your thoughtfulness," Dani said. "Thank you."

"We will work together to make sure she's taken care of," Skyler said.

Chance hurried out, returning a few moments later accompanying a petite woman with long auburn hair. She smiled at Dani.

"Hey, Ayla. Great to see you." Tiandra crossed the room to hug the newcomer.

Dani approached with an outstretched hand. "Dani Fontaine."

"Nice to meet you," Ayla said, her expression softening as she glanced at the playpen.

The sounds of cooing had Dani hurrying to retrieve Tessa. She held her up and turned to face Ayla.

"And this must be darling Tessa."

In response, the infant blew spit bubbles, entertaining herself.

"May I?" Ayla asked.

"You don't mind?"

"Are you kidding?" Ayla chuckled. "This is a great break from dealing with criminal cases."

Dani gently passed off Tessa.

"Ayla understands the trauma of being a witness in need of protection." Chance smiled at his spouse. The adoration written on his face spoke of love.

"Right? I'm happy to help after all this team did for me," Ayla said.

Dani wondered at their story, but with all that was happening, she put a pin in the question. "You guys are amazing." She forced back the tears threatening to erupt. She couldn't deny the bond she already felt with HFTF. This incredible group led by the one man who had stolen her heart so many years before.

"It's what family does." Tiandra gave her a wink.

Family. The small word held power. Hadn't Jayne referenced their friendship that way, too?

Walsh moved near Ayla, then pivoted before exiting the conference room.

Had the others noticed how he avoided Tessa? For

the first time, Dani considered the possibility that he didn't like kids.

Eliana gasped and jumped to her feet without saying a word. She hurried from the Rock.

"What was that about?" Elijah asked.

Through the walled glass, they watched as she rushed into Walsh's office. The two quickly returned to the Rock.

"The weapons destruction consultant is Aiden De-Luca," Eliana announced to the group.

"Should that mean something to us?" Chance asked.

"It does to me," Walsh replied. "Is his name familiar to any of you?"

"Vaguely." Skyler placed a finger against her lips, in thought.

"Aiden DeLuca is a former Omaha PD officer," Walsh advised. "He sustained permanent damage to his shoulder after a suspect shot him during a call. He took an early retirement."

"Wow, that's harsh," Chance said.

"I wouldn't wish that on anybody," Graham agreed.

"Aiden's got a solid reputation in the law enforcement community," Walsh explained.

"He started a new career as a weapons destruction expert?" Riker surmised.

"Yes," Walsh replied. "I haven't talked with him in a long time." Something flashed over his expression, then disappeared just as quickly, leaving Dani curious.

"Regardless if Aiden was a stand-up guy, a life-changing injury could provide a catalyst for behavior transformation," Eliana said.

"It would destroy his entire identity without warning," Walsh replied.

"Let's not venture down this road yet," Elijah said.

"True." Skyler nodded. "We'll take the information into consideration."

"Eliana, run a background on Aiden DeLuca and update us," Walsh instructed. "Dani and I will interview him."

"Roger that." Eliana's fingers danced over the keyboard.

Dani stepped toward Ayla. "Tessa's diaper bag has whatever you'll need." She glanced over her shoulder at Eliana. "Thanks to Eliana's quick and generous thinking."

The tech smiled at her. "My pleasure."

Ayla got Tessa settled with some toys in the playpen, talking to her while Eliana collected data on the weapons consultant. Within minutes, she announced, "Sent his LKA to your phones."

Dani's phone pinged with the Last Known Address for Aiden DeLuca and his driver's license picture. He didn't look familiar to her, but that wasn't unexpected. "Knox, ready?"

The Dobie mix looked up from his position next to Destiny, then got to his feet and strolled to Dani.

She snapped on his leash. "After the bombing at the Ibarras' home, I'm not leaving Knox behind."

"Agreed. We could've used his nose the other

night," Walsh responded. "We'll also search Jayne's residence."

Dani debated asking for a delay, considering nothing thus far had fallen in Jayne's favor. Secretly, she feared what else they'd find. But they'd put off the inevitable too long. It was time for them to go. An idea bounded to mind. "We need a warrant."

"Already secured," Riker said.

Dani whipped her head in Walsh's direction in a silent demand for an explanation. "It's a normal part of the investigation." He shrugged.

Everything within her wanted to argue, but he was right. Still, she didn't like the thought of strangers going through Jayne's possessions. "Could we conduct the search after we visit DeLuca? I'd like to swing by my place again, too. I'd like to pick up a few more things." She'd been in a hurry when they'd gone the first time and neglected to grab her running shoes and workout clothes.

"Absolutely," Walsh replied.

Relieved to have some control over the situation, Dani focused her attention on her canine. "C'mon, Knox, road trip." The Dobie mix wagged his stubby tail, conveying his eagerness to work.

The other dogs rose with him, barking and tails wagging. All watching expectantly for their handlers to leash them.

"Not yet, Bosco," Tiandra cooed, stroking the Malinois' head.

Ammo sauntered toward Riker, nudging his hand. "You started a dog riot," Riker teased.

Dani winced. "Sorry about that."

"I'll assist Elijah and Graham at GIPD, too, and work on the missing evidence search," Chance said.

"Good." Walsh exited the conference room.

Dani would need Jayne's keys to enter her apartment. If the team broke down the door, they'd attract the neighbors' unwanted attention. She called Nancy, the nurse she'd spoken to several times since Jayne's admission. "The medics secured Jayne's purse with her belongings when you admitted her. I'd like to pick that up for safekeeping."

"Of course, when you get here, ask for me," Nancy replied. "I'll ensure it's released into your custody."

"Thank you." They disconnected, and Dani looked up, meeting everyone's compassionate stares.

"We'll continue praying," Eliana promised.

Skyler touched Dani's arm. "Don't give up hope."

"No time like the present." Walsh returned to the room.

The group surrounded Dani, lifting their voices. Petitions for wisdom over Dani and Walsh, the team's safety, Jayne's healing, and justice in the case, humbled Dani. She blinked back tears at the collective amens that filled the Rock and their genuine concern.

"The hospital is first on the route, so let's start there," Walsh said. He understood Dani's desire to stall the search in Jayne's apartment, and he'd done his best to give her time to come to terms with the inevitable.

He'd acquiesced, but the mounting evidence forced

his hand. He expected Dani to unleash on him about obtaining the warrant without her approval, but it seemed she realized they couldn't avoid protocol. Perhaps her experience working in command had taught her the difficulties of following rules, regardless of the cost to one's personal relationships. Maybe they'd both learned a lot since Walsh's investigation of Chief Varmose. Him to be more understanding and her to put the job ahead of her feelings.

Once they reached the hospital, Dani secured Knox's department-issued halter. With the identification, there wouldn't be issues taking him inside. The intense summer heat was too much for him to be left in the vehicle.

They rode the elevator in silence. Knox seemed to sense Dani's stress. He nudged her hand and offered a compassionate gaze from his dark eyes. Walsh envied the quiet understanding that passed between them without words.

"He gets you."

She nodded. "Yeah, truthfully, Knox is more comfort dog than K-9," Dani replied, absently stroking the animal's short coat. "He's such a softie at heart."

When they reached the floor where Jayne had been transferred and admitted, they strolled to the nurses' station. A short woman with Nancy on her name badge was waiting for them. "Chief, it's nice to meet you in person."

"This is Commander Beckham Walsh," Dani introduced him as he shook the nurse's hand.

"The state troopers guarding your friend are very kind," Nancy led them down the hallway.

Walsh noted the nurse didn't speak Jayne's name aloud. Captain Bonn had advised that aside from the security detail, only Nancy—as the head nurse—would be aware of Jayne's real identity. As they approached the trooper on duty, he rose from the chair positioned in front of the door.

"Commander Walsh and Chief Fontaine." Walsh extended a hand.

"Trooper Nguyen."

"We won't be long," Walsh assured him.

Nancy released the lock with her badge, allowing them to enter. "I'll give you privacy and bring the items you requested." The door shut softly behind them.

Tubes and wires streamed from the unconscious woman. Her pale skin and dark hair contrasted the white pillowcase.

Walsh stepped back, giving Dani space. She slowly eased around the bed, passing him Knox's leash. The dog dropped to sit beside him.

Dani gently swept loose strands from Jayne's face. She placed her hands on the railing and closed her eyes. Walsh felt like an intruder on a private moment, but unsure where else to be, he remained silent, watching. Dani never spoke, but slowly swiped at a stray tear streaming down her cheek.

Nancy returned and handed Dani a plastic bag with the hospital's logo on the front.

"Thank you," Dani said. "We should go." She led the way out.

Walsh addressed Nguyen, and he and Dani exited the hospital, not speaking to one another.

After loading Knox into Walsh's temporary replacement pickup, Dani slid into the passenger seat. "I appreciate you staying with me."

Stunned and humbled, Walsh passed her a pair of latex gloves. He'd expected Dani to admonish him for the lack of privacy. Instead, she'd thanked him for accompanying her.

She opened the bag and withdrew Jayne's purse, examining the contents. "I'll do a thorough inventory when we get to my office." Finding nothing of consequence, Dani replaced the items into the bag. "At least we have her keys. I don't want to ignite nosy neighbor rumors."

"I understand this is hard…" Walsh began.

Dani shook her head. "Let's focus on the case, okay?" She withdrew her phone, starting the GPS for Aiden's address. "DeLuca's place isn't far from here."

Walsh eyed the directions, started the engine, and headed westbound on Interstate 80.

Aiden's home sat on the edge of Gretna, a suburb west of Omaha. They pulled up to the modest, two-story building with a single garage, which sat in an older but well-maintained neighborhood. Walsh surveyed the structure, noticing the drapes were closed, prohibiting them from seeing inside.

He parked, and they exited the vehicle. Dani

leashed Knox, then trailed Walsh up the sidewalk to the front door.

He rapped twice.

Silence.

Walsh pressed the doorbell.

Again, no response.

"Mr. DeLuca?" Walsh called.

Dani tried the number Eliana had provided for Aiden. "The line rang several times before transferring to an automated voicemail."

"Few people have landlines anymore. It's possible a cell phone is his only mode of communication."

"Something seems off," Dani said.

"Let's check around back."

They walked the perimeter of the house to a six-foot privacy fence that portioned off the yard. A gate to the right of the driveway stood ajar. Walsh pushed it open, and they entered the backyard. An older model grill sat on the square concrete porch where several lawn chairs were positioned next to a table with a dilapidated umbrella, leaning precariously to one side.

Walsh watched as Knox sniffed the area. "What's he doing?" The hairs rose on Walsh's neck.

"He's showing interest, but not alerting."

"Interpretation, please?" Walsh scanned the windows facing them.

"We're not in danger. At least not by explosives."

"Thanks for that clarification," Walsh grumbled.

An old gas mower was pushed against the shed. Overgrown sections of grass and weeds in the unkempt yard said someone had started landscaping work and never finished.

A screen door at the rear side of the house also stood ajar.

"Mr. DeLuca?" Walsh glanced at Dani and gestured toward the entrance. She gave a curt nod.

Both armed, they moved into a stack position.

Walsh pointed to a rust-colored smear on the door-frame. Blood.

"Mr. DeLuca," he called again, inching the door wider with the toe of his boot.

"Police," Dani added, tugging Knox closer to her right leg.

They stepped into the kitchen, where a mound of dirty dishes covered the countertop and overflowed into the sink. Flies buzzed overhead.

Someone had pulled out the drawers, and the cabinet doors stood wide open. All the contents were tossed haplessly onto the floor. Indication of a search.

They made their way to the living room adjacent to the dining area. The disorder continued. The intruder had ripped cushions off the sofa, scattered pictures and sports memorabilia across the carpet.

Walsh shifted closer to the coffee table, which was broken in the center. "Clear signs of a struggle."

"Mr. DeLuca, police!"

She and Walsh turned their backs to one another as they inched through the hallway, clearing the bedrooms and bathrooms on both sides. Every room was in shambles. When they'd cleared the house, they holstered their guns.

"I'll call it in." Dani reached for her phone.

Walsh scanned the living room. Pictures of Aiden, with whom he assumed were friends and family, lay on the floor. He squatted to gain a better look. A younger version of the Aiden DeLuca he'd remembered stood proudly while an older woman with similar features pinned his badge.

Dark stains on the gray carpet got his attention. "Hey, Dani?"

She walked over and knelt beside him. Walsh pointed to blood droplets that led to the front door.

"Well, this changes things."

"And as of right now, we're classifying DeLuca as a missing person."

"He's a suspect," Dani corrected. "I checked the garage and there's no vehicle there."

"Yes, he's a person of interest, just like Jayne," he said. "I'll request an APB for him and his last registered vehicle," Walsh said, referencing the all-points bulletin. The sound of screeching tires carried to them.

Knox lunged, barking at the entrance.

An eerie silence fell. Then rapid gunfire shattered the front window. Walsh dove, tackling Dani and Knox simultaneously to the floor. They rolled toward the hallway as rounds pelted the drywall, shattering pictures, and glass around them.

Walsh gripped his phone and called 9-1-1, shouting into the receiver, "Shots fired, shots fired!"

# EIGHT

The firestorm seemed to come from every direction in an unending cacophony of blasts. Walsh stayed in a crouch, Dani beside him. He dropped his phone into his breast pocket, unable to hear the dispatcher's response. He prayed help was on the way.

Both prepared to return fire, but the relentless attack offered no opening. Glass and drywall exploded around them, filling the space in a cloud of debris. Dani hovered over Knox, protecting him.

Then, as quickly as it began, the firefight ceased abruptly, followed by squealing tires. Walsh moved to the window and peered out. Thankfully, the shooter hadn't destroyed the temporary SUV he'd driven. One minute advantage.

He helped Dani to her feet, and they visually assessed the damage.

"Someone doesn't want us to find the connection," she said.

"Yeah." Walsh's instincts told him there was a lot more to the case than missing weapons. With three suspects in the mix, things had grown increasingly complicated.

At last local PD arrived. Walsh and Dani exited through the back door, not wanting to disturb any potential evidence.

They approached the two patrol units, and Walsh

offered a rundown of the events and requested crime scene processing.

The officers took the report and once they'd assumed command, Walsh, Dani, and Knox headed out.

Walsh called the tech. "Eliana, please provide a group update to the team." Again, he provided a synopsis of what had occurred.

"Got it," she said.

"Look for details on Aiden DeLuca's registered vehicle."

"Will do. I'll be in touch."

They disconnected, and Walsh merged onto Highway 80 eastbound.

Within minutes, Eliana texted him with the information.

Using his speakerphone feature, Walsh called Captain Bonn. "Need your help," he blurted before Bonn said hello. "Could you please issue an APB for Aiden DeLuca and an older model Ford F-150. Tan with Nebraska license plates." He rattled off the plate number.

"I'll get it handled," Bonn replied, hanging up.

Walsh's phone rang, and he again answered on speakerphone. "Chance, are you in GI?"

"Yes, sir," Chance replied. "We found something interesting and need you to come here ASAP."

"We're on our way," Walsh advised.

"See you soon." He disconnected.

"The evidence at Aiden's doesn't prove he was in cahoots with Jayne," Dani said, "but whoever shot at us is most likely the same person who has him."

"True. However, Aiden's reputation in the law enforcement community is solid. I suspect foul play."

"I'm not disagreeing with you, but I believe there's more to the story than Jayne dishing out evidence," Dani countered.

Walsh considered his words. "I get the need to be loyal to your team. You've met mine. I'd lay my life on the line for any of them without a second thought."

Her eyes drilled through him.

Walsh braced for her argument of his next statement. "Perhaps you'll want to recuse yourself. Focus on taking care of Tessa."

Dani crossed her arms. "I knew you'd say that."

"I'm not implying you're incapable of handling this investigation. I'm simply saying I'm aware that eliminating your personal feelings isn't always achievable."

"Beckham Walsh, you might have issues with that, but I do not. I'm a professional. First and foremost, a cop."

"As am I."

"Then you understand that partiality isn't allowable. Yes, I believe in Jayne's innocence, but not because I'm ignoring the evidence. I've seen her day-to-day work ethics. There is nothing substantial linking Jayne to the missing weapons."

"There is plenty of evidence," Walsh contended.

"All circumstantial," Dani corrected. "And we cannot arrest or charge her purely based upon that. If, and/or when, we find proof of her involvement, we will handle it at that time, and not assume it beforehand."

Walsh sighed. A twinge of guilt pricked at him. Not so long ago, he'd faced a similar situation with Riker. Additionally, he'd told Dani they'd not jump to conclusions about Aiden's involvement. He had to extend that same courtesy to Jayne. Admittedly, he'd not questioned Riker's innocence, regardless of the evidence stacked against him. "Maybe it has nothing to do with her personally. Could be a group targeting smaller agencies or enemies of HFTF seeking revenge," Walsh said.

The remainder of the drive was quiet until they pulled into the GIPD parking lot and exited the vehicle.

If he wasn't imagining it, Dani appeared on edge with him. He fought the urge to reach over and squeeze her hand, reminding her they were on the same side, allies, not enemies. He sighed, hating the contention that lingered between them like an unwanted guest.

They walked into the building, greeted professionally by officers and personnel. However, Walsh didn't miss the aloofness they all exhibited. Understandably so.

"Might as well talk with Chance first." Dani led him to the evidence storage area.

Chance stood beside a worktable, wearing a somber expression.

"Your face tells me we won't like what you have to say," Walsh said.

"Yeah…we've sorted through the records for our stored evidence and there's an issue." He passed a paper to Walsh and Dani. They both leaned forward to read.

Walsh immediately spotted the color difference in the ink. Similar, but different, and not authentic to the original writing. The same person had changed the inventory numbers too. "Someone falsified the records," he said.

"Yes, sir, and the numbers do not match the inventory. Furthermore, someone compromised the evidence tape that sealed the containers, then tried covering their tracks." Chance pointed to a box on the side counter. "At first glance, it wasn't obvious. Upon closer inspection, we confirmed the sections were tampered with." He stepped back, stroking Destiny, who panted softly beside him.

"Jayne would've secured the tape after logging the items into the evidence locker," Dani explained. "If someone requested to get into the sealed box, they'd have to sign the log and the original binding to establish the chain of custody."

"Right," Walsh agreed. "But this document shows those steps weren't followed."

"This isn't the only one." Chance passed his cell phone to Walsh.

The device showed a box that HFTF had logged into evidence several months prior. Walsh expanded the picture and spotted the severed tape. He handed the device to Dani.

"That's impossible." Dani zoomed in on the screen and her cheeks reddened. She opened her mouth, then clamped it shut again. "I'm speechless." She lowered her arm, setting Chance's phone on the table.

"Chance, thank you for the update. Please continue the work," Walsh said. "Dani and I will be in her office before heading to Jayne's apartment."

The younger marshal gave a curt nod as they exited the room.

Once they were in Dani's office with her door closed, she perched on the edge of her desk. "Don't say it."

"Evidence speaks for itself."

At her glower, he lifted his hands in surrender. "It's time we went through Jayne's things." He'd not pushed the issue with the chain of events, but he couldn't delay any longer.

Dani nodded consent. "Before we go, let's check Jayne's locker."

They moved to the main office where a husky man sat behind a desk with a sign on the door that read HR Manager. She didn't introduce Walsh, so he hesitated, listening.

"I need Jayne Bardot's personnel file and the key to her locker," Dani said.

The manager shot a look at Walsh but didn't question the order. He got to his feet, returning with a manila folder. "Chief."

"Thank you," she said curtly before walking out.

Walsh followed Dani to her office and settled at the small conference table. She placed the folder between them, and they sorted through the documents. Nothing seemed out of the ordinary. There were no disciplinary actions. Her file proclaimed the opposite. Jayne was an exemplary evidence technician.

"Unless you see something here that I don't," Dani said, "I'd say the information confirms what I've said from the start."

"She appears to be a stellar employee. On paper."

"She is." Dani rose. "Let's check her locker."

They walked through the building to an ajar door marked by a sign that read Women's Locker Room. Women's voices carried out to the hallway.

"They should be out shortly. It's close to shift change." Dani leaned against the wall.

The voices grew louder, as the speakers neared where Walsh and Dani waited.

"Heard that task force is here doing an IA," a woman said, referencing an internal affairs investigation.

A second added, "Rumor is Jayne Bardot's somehow involved."

Dani cringed, saddened by her personnel discussing the situation. Yet, what did she expect? That was human nature.

She didn't recognize the speakers, but then she was still new to the agency.

"I never trusted Jayne. She's too close to the chief. Figure she's a plant spying for Fontaine," the first woman replied.

Dani's ears warmed, disheartened at their opinions of her. The moment triggered emotions from the years after Walsh arrested Chief Varmose. Her fellow officers had shunned her then too.

She lingered, hating herself for eavesdropping, then reasoned this was a fact-finding mission. Would they say anything to help with the case, since they were unaware she and Walsh were listening in?

Walsh worked his jaw, apparently unimpressed with the chatter.

"Yeah, wonder what this means for the chief?" the second woman asked. "Can't be good for that kind of accusation this early on her watch."

Dani's stomach plummeted straight to her boots. She glanced down. Losing the confidence of her officers would be a detrimental obstacle to overcome. All this time, she'd worried about Jayne's involvement in the case, completely ignoring how the situation affected her own job.

"That K-9 officer from the Heartland Fugitive Task Force is easy on the eyes," the first commented, changing topics.

Dani met Walsh's gaze, and he gave a slight shake of his head, realizing the speaker meant Chance Tavalla. She thought of his kind wife, Ayla, who was taking care of Tessa, and sent up a prayer of gratitude.

The door swung open, revealing the speakers. Olga, the receptionist, stepped back startled, colliding with GIPD officer, Yessinia Zarick, who blurted, "Hi, Chief." The young officer's wide eyes spoke surprise, resembling a teenager caught sneaking in after curfew. "Oh hi, Knox." Her joyful tone didn't match her embarrassed expression.

Knox harrumphed, moving closer to Dani. She recognized Yessinia as the speaker beaming about Chance.

"Good morning, Chief," Olga parroted, leaning against the doorframe in an attempt at a casual response, while her countenance mirrored the same guilt as Yessinia's.

"Ladies," Dani replied. "How was your workout?" She glanced at her watch pointedly, reminding them they needed to get to work.

"Excellent." Olga's face was so red she looked like she might spontaneously combust in place.

Yessinia swallowed hard. "Well, I gotta get ready for shift change."

"Have a great day!" Olga bounced behind her, and the women quickly exited the locker room.

"Shall we?" Dani peered inside the room, avoiding Walsh's eyes. Once she'd confirmed it was empty, they entered, propping the door open.

"Are you okay?" Walsh asked.

"Guess their candid comments shouldn't shock me," Dani said, leading the way to Jayne's personal locker. Knox remained at her side.

As the new chief, she should expect her personnel to pretend to be kind to her face while talking behind her back about the issues of command staff. The overwhelming evidence against Jayne weighed on Dani. Though she longed to argue plausible reasons in her friend's favor, truthfully, her own assurances quavered.

She'd never admit that to Walsh.

Not yet anyway.

Dani exhaled, then inserted the key into Jayne's assigned locker. She tugged open the door and stepped to the side, allowing Walsh to see the contents: workout shorts and a tank top sat atop a pair of running shoes. She remembered Jayne often came in early, taking advantage of the exercise facilities.

Donning gloves Walsh handed her, Dani removed the evidence bag she'd stuffed into her pocket. She lifted the items carefully to check deeper inside the space. A makeup pouch filled with toiletries was hidden beneath the clothes. Dani sorted through, feeling like the worst kind of intruder.

Would it matter if she had to arrest her friend?

Dani paused and withdrew a piece of paper sticking out of a compact mirror case. It was a picture of Jayne with Aiden DeLuca. Dani's heart raced, and she lifted the photo higher up to the light. It was a photo-booth shot, like those taken at a mall kiosk. Jayne smiled for the camera, while Aiden planted a kiss on her cheek.

Nausea overwhelmed Dani. Jayne not only knew Aiden but was also in a relationship with him. On the back was written *Love you, babe*.

Dani's stomach twisted with hurt and anger. She leaned hard against the locker, passing the incriminating evidence. How had she been so wrong about Jayne?

Her mind raced with the implications. Had Jayne used Dani, gaining her trust and her position to obtain access to the weapons, then conspired with Aiden to steal them? If so, why was he missing? Had they gotten wrapped up with Enrique Prachank? Dani wanted to believe there was a reasonable explanation. But she couldn't deny the proof in front of her.

Even if both were casualties of a poor decision, they were romantically involved. That wouldn't bode well with HFTF.

Conviction rose within Dani. Ridiculous as it might sound, she believed there was more to the story. Jayne wouldn't risk custody of Tessa without a valid explanation. Jayne's participation could've been involuntary.

"Let's move to your office for privacy," Walsh suggested, breaking the silence.

Dani nodded, secured the locker, and trailed him out of the room.

*Lord, what do I do?*

Walsh closed the door, and they settled at her conference table. Knox sat beside her, laying his head in her lap. "Hey buddy." She stroked his soft coat.

The task force already believed Jayne was guilty. The picture would solidify their assumptions. They'd pursue the path to charge her with the missing evidence. Yet she'd called Dani to meet with her, asking for help. She'd even gone as far as to hide Tessa in the closet and ask Dani to care for the infant if necessary.

People made mistakes and simple things got out of hand. She'd seen it all the time in law enforcement. She had to believe the best about Jayne. If she'd deceived Dani, and Jayne had used her, then their entire friendship was fake.

And that meant Dani was a fool. Just like when she'd ignored the signs of her husband's shifting priorities though he claimed he didn't need more than a career-seeking wife. Mark had promised a life without kids was enough for him. Then he'd left her for another woman and had the family he'd claimed he never wanted from her.

Before that, she'd ignored the truth about her commanding chief—a horrible, conniving criminal. She'd defended Varmose to the end, destroying her relationship with Walsh and enduring the hatred of her fellow officers.

Dani couldn't be that naïve ever again.

She sighed.

"Let's talk it out." Walsh's even tone and tender expression tore at Dani's heart.

"What if Aiden used Jayne to get the munitions? Perhaps he'd convinced her to help him steal them? After all, your team found guns that were logged in his possession—weapons he was supposed to have destroyed."

"Plausible." Walsh leaned back.

Encouraged, Dani added. "What if he threatened or betrayed Jayne? She might've played a part in the crimes, but if it was under coercion or fear for her life or Tessa's, that explains a lot."

And that sounded much more like the Jayne Dani knew.

"Okay, let's follow up on DeLuca and notify the team of the finding," Walsh replied. "Trust the system and the process to reveal the truth."

Dani nodded mutely. More so, she had to trust God to handle it all because it was far beyond her abilities. "You make the calls. I need to give Knox a break outside."

She rose and hurried from the room.

Dani took a side exit. She needed a second to gather her thoughts and pray. The photo weighed like a fifty-pound cannon ball on her heart.

Standing on the front lawn of her department, Dani contemplated the totality of events. For the first time, she got honest with herself. Walsh had hurt her by hiding Varmose's investigation, but she understood why he'd done it. The pain of betrayal remained, though she might never confess that to Walsh. Just as Jayne had to understand Dani's responsibility to investigate this case, regardless of their friendship. Funny how history had repeated itself. She'd walked out of a situation where she'd trusted someone immensely, only to have egg on her face.

Worse, Beckham Walsh was there to witness her mistakes.

Again.

# NINE

"Got any updates on Aiden DeLuca?" Walsh asked when Captain Bonn answered his call.

"Negative on DeLuca. Crime scene techs completed a thorough workup on the house. They found nothing beyond the blood droplets and smear you reported." Bonn continued, "We're waiting on DNA to confirm whether the sample is DeLuca's."

"There wasn't a significant amount."

"Correct. Most likely a minor wound. Forced entry into the house. No missing valuables, so we ruled out robbery."

Walsh recalled seeing electronics and cash on the nightstand at Aiden's place. "I appreciate it."

Bonn disconnected. A glance at his watch had Walsh concerned. He'd already called in HFTF, and Dani hadn't yet returned. After all she'd endured, she probably wanted alone time. Away from him.

A rap on the door got his attention.

"Come in."

Chance entered, Destiny at his side. The K-9 strode to Walsh for a quick petting before curling up on Knox's bed.

"Eliana updated me on the picture." Chance dropped onto the chair opposite him. "Does the word 'Decorah' mean anything to you?"

"No. Never heard of it."

"It's a small town in the northeastern part of Iowa."

Dani entered with Knox and the Dobie mix rushed to Destiny. The German shepherd glanced up lazily and offered a few thumps of her tail. Knox settled beside her, and both emitted contented sighs.

"Guess those two bonded." Dani smiled but it never reached her eyes. She sat next to Chance. "Why do you ask?"

Chance flashed Walsh a look, the silent request for permission to continue talking in front of her.

Fleeting annoyance shadowed Dani's face and Walsh gave an imperceptible nod.

"A receipt for a Decorah coffeehouse was in Jayne's desk." Chance passed the slip sealed in a plastic zipper bag to Dani. "Did she have family or friends there?"

"I don't think so." Dani tilted her head, studying the paper.

"Hmm. Seems strange." Chance reached for the bag.

"Hold on." Dani snapped a picture with her cell phone. "Maybe she had a weekend away."

The verbal dismissal didn't match the deceit Walsh detected in her response. Had he imagined it?

"Consider everything," Walsh said.

"Agreed." Dani sighed, steepling her fingers. "It was the only out-of-place part of her workspace that we've found so far. Jayne's meticulous."

The anomaly stood out. Accidental? Or had Jayne left it on purpose?

"We'll check her schedule for any recent travels," Chance said.

"I don't deal with her daily assignments, so I'm unaware when she comes and goes." Dani's posture conveyed defensiveness, though her tone remained light.

"Eliana will dig into Jayne's financials and see if she can tap into her phone's GPS as well." Chance pushed away from the table. "We'll keep you updated." He walked to the door, gesturing for Destiny. The shepherd opened an eye but stayed curled beside Knox.

"She's welcome to stay here," Dani said.

"Thanks." Chance put his hands into his pockets, hesitating. "Um, one last thing."

Dani and Walsh shared a look before offering him their full attention. Chance had become more secure in their discussions, but he lacked the confidence Walsh wanted him to exude when on duty.

Did he intimidate the marshal? If so, why? He'd offered support and encouragement. Walsh recognized his rough edges sometimes came off harshly.

"The county attorney's office called…" Chance began, referencing Ayla's employer. "Eliana is at the Rock with Tessa, but Ayla has to go back to work overtime on a case."

"She's a paralegal," Walsh explained to Dani.

Understanding swept over her expression. "Oh, sure! I appreciate all you've done." She smiled and started to rise.

Walsh gestured for her to relax.

"I'm missing Tessa. We'll return to Omaha immediately."

"No rush." Relief covered Chance's face. "Eliana said not to worry. It's all good."

"That sounds like her." Walsh chuckled. "I'll advise our ETA after we search Jayne's residence."

Dani frowned. Was she hoping to postpone it?

Chance squatted in front of Destiny and whispered, "Be back soon. Relax here." She thumped her feathery tail in reply. "Holler if you want me to get her," Chance added.

"No problem," Dani replied with a smile.

Chance left the office, closing the door behind him.

Before Walsh could speak, Dani blurted, "I'm sorry for the extra work Tessa has put on your team. They're not babysitters. I don't expect them to behave as such. Perhaps we could call in protective detail from another agency?"

"That's a great idea." Before she changed her mind, Walsh called Nebraska State Patrol Captain Bonn.

The line rang twice before he answered. "We've never talked this much in such a short amount of time."

"Seriously." Walsh smirked. "I have a request." He provided a brief explanation and asked for troopers to assist with Tessa's protection at headquarters. "If possible, have them meet us at the Rock first thing in the morning."

"Expect them," Bonn replied.

"I owe you."

"Happy to help." They disconnected.

Dani looked up, a light shimmer in her eyes. "Thank you." She glanced at the photo of Jayne and Aiden DeLuca.

Walsh scooted closer. "You walked in here looking like you'd witnessed a train wreck."

"That's not too far off as analogies go."

He lifted the photo and fought to maintain a stoic expression. "I must admit, I didn't expect to find this."

"There's a reasonable explanation." Dani reiterated her belief that Jayne had been coerced somehow.

Walsh stifled his irritation and impatience, quirking an eyebrow in silent protest.

Dani rambled on, undeterred by his obvious skepticism. "Until we're certain, we have to keep an open mind."

Walsh weighed his next words. "No argument there, but this is totally reaching."

"I resent that." Dani sat back, crossing her arms. Several seconds passed and her defensive posture faded. "No, I don't. You're right. Just please don't give up on Jayne until we uncover the truth."

"You have my word." Walsh leaned forward. "What else has you rattled?"

She averted her eyes. "I debated taking the chief position here. I didn't have a history with the department and wasn't sure they'd receive me since I hadn't risen through their ranks."

"I get that."

"Earning my personnel's trust is huge."

"Unquestionably." Walsh thought of his group. They'd worked together, creating the solid bond.

"You haven't had that issue with your task force. They're amazing."

"Every new commander contends with challenges,"

Walsh corrected her. "The trust and confidence team members have with one another doesn't happen overnight. It takes time to build up to the level HFTF has now. I'm grateful for the incredible privilege God has offered to me in leading them."

"Your faith bonds you."

"Yes. It doesn't fix all our problems, but it provides a solid cornerstone. That's why we call our conference room the Rock and start every case in prayer." Walsh glanced down. "You're the one who inspired my faith."

Dani blinked. "Me?"

"Absolutely. It has always been one of your most attractive traits." Realizing his confession, he quickly reversed topics. "Your personnel will come around."

"For this to happen early in my career as a chief is rough. I cannot believe their insinuation that I sent Jayne in as a spy for me." Dani rolled her eyes. "As though I have the time to orchestrate nefarious plans."

Walsh crossed one ankle over his knee.

"Although Olga and Yissinia were complimentary of Chance." Dani leaned back and he acknowledged her efforts to divert the discussion.

"They'd never drag him away from Ayla." Walsh stifled a grin. "He's as loyal as they come."

She smiled. "She's a blessed woman. Men like him are a rare and precious find."

Walsh wondered at her comment, realizing he knew little of her personal life after their falling out. But now wasn't the time to ask. "Does Jayne have friends here?"

The team had questioned the personnel. So far, no one had claimed to be close to the evidence tech.

"She confessed I was her only friend," Dani said. "Painful, considering she never mentioned Aiden De-Luca."

"That puts you in an awkward situation as her boss," Walsh surmised.

"I thought I was handling it well. Apparently, I was wrong."

Walsh tamped down his anger, recalling the women's locker room conversation. The urge to deal with their hateful comments warred within him. Dani was perfectly capable of defending herself, but he longed to assume that role for her.

"Not only are they questioning my authority and competency, but I don't blame them."

Shocked by the heartfelt confession, Walsh assured her, "This isn't your fault."

He hated that Jayne had put Dani in the difficult position. And in typical Dani fashion, she'd willingly fall on her sword to protect her friend.

Walsh added, "Jayne made her own choices."

"What if they were ultimatums?"

The woman's relentless hope, though inspiring, wore on Walsh. He pointed to the picture. "This proves they were in a relationship. Regardless of the hows and whys, why not come to you if she'd gotten in too deep?"

"That's exactly why she asked me to meet her. She might've had evidence to give us then," Dani contended. "That paints Aiden as the warehouse shooter. He tried to stop her from ratting him out."

"Okay, suppose that's true. Where is he now?"

"Simple. He took off when his plan didn't work. He's afraid of being caught."

"Why was his house ransacked? He could've skipped town without adding that detail. And they found blood evidence."

Dani waved him off. "That's an easy plant."

"If Aiden's a victim, Jayne might've played him."

Her jaw hardened, but she didn't argue. "I suppose there's probability in your scenario," she conceded. "If she doesn't recover, we'll never know."

Walsh reached out a hand to comfort her but stopped before making contact. He needed to keep his professional distance. "On that note, have you considered the next steps with Tessa should Jayne's condition continue to decline?"

"Yes, sort of." Dani blew out a long breath. "I can't go there yet. The tiny thread of hope I'm clinging to is the only thing keeping me from completely unraveling."

Walsh understood her point of view far better than he dared to share.

Dani stood in Jayne's living room. They'd entered the residence without drawing the attention of Jayne's nosy neighbors, but they might not leave with the same results.

"Divide and conquer?" Walsh asked.

"Yeah." She faced Knox. "Stay."

The dog dropped into a regal sphinx position at the door.

Dani paused in the familiar space, surveying it through an investigator's eyes. The love seat sat opposite a console table holding a TV and framed pictures of Tessa. Dani fingered the delicate threads of the hand-embroidered pillows placed on the sofa. Dani agreed Jayne had a talent for the hobby. Tessa's baby swing stood beside the window and a carousel toy lay on the floor. Everything in the house attested to a devoted mother who doted on her only child. She strolled to Jayne's bedroom.

Walsh was digging through the dresser's contents.

Taking his lead, she tugged open the nightstand drawer. Inside lay a Bible, a piece of paper peeking out from the center, beside a women's devotional. Dani extracted it. The same name of the Decorah coffee shop Chance had found on a receipt earlier was printed at the top. Centered was a hand drawn sketch of a cube and half-rounded triangle.

Walsh approached her, and she passed it to him. "Looks like doodling."

"Doubtful."

Dani captured a photo, then bagged the item for evidence.

They perused the rest of the apartment, finding nothing incriminating, to her relief. Dani said, "We should scoot to Omaha. C'mon Knox." Dani ushered Walsh out the door and locked it.

Dani drifting to sleep on the return trip, waking as Walsh pulled into HFTF's underground garage.

Eliana met them with Tessa, allowing them to get to the condo faster.

Dani studied the picture on her phone of the drawing from Jayne's apartment. "I thought it was a triangle, but it's round." She opened her internet browser and searched Decorah attractions. Immediately, one got her attention. "It's the ice caves in Palisades Park!"

"Great work!" Walsh commended.

Knox pushed his head between the seats, joining the discussion. Tessa cooed from the backseat, happily swatting at a hanging toy from her carrier. Grateful they'd taken out the seat at the Ibarras' before the explosion, Dani sent up a prayer of thanks.

"Why sketch it instead of writing the words?" Dani asked.

"What's an ice cave hundreds of miles from Grand Island, Nebraska, got to do with Jayne?"

"We must check it out," Dani said.

"It's late. Let's make the drive first thing in the morning after we meet with the troopers handling Tessa's protection detail."

"Okay. Thank you again for handling that."

Walsh didn't look her way. He most likely feared she'd explode. "You're a fantastic investigator. Jayne needs your skills now."

She exhaled. "This is all new to me."

"Did you want the husband, children, house with a picket fence, and a dog?" Walsh's tone held a teasing element.

Dani met his unwavering gaze for several seconds. "You don't have to—"

"I married my career. Balancing a family and a high-intensity job isn't a viable option. You can't serve two masters."

"Actually, if you're referencing the Bible verse, I think Jesus meant money," Walsh replied lightly.

"It's true. Something will take precedent." Against her mind warning her to stop talking, she blurted, "I never told you this when we were dating, but my father abandoned my mom and me. He chose another woman and then had a family with her. Mom instantly became a single parent. She did her best to balance her surgical career and me, but I felt like an inconvenience. I vowed to never put a child in that position."

Walsh gaped at her. "That must've been awful."

"It was a life lesson for me." She glanced down. "I'm grateful I learned it early on."

She'd fought a male-dominated vocation. Always having to be twice as good, competent, and skilled. No criminal would take that away.

Walsh pulled into the condo's parking lot and Dani threw open her door. "Let's finish this. It's cost me too much to get this far."

# TEN

Orange and purple splashed the sky with the sunrise the following day. Dani and Knox trailed Walsh through the HFTF building to the elevators.

"Captain Bonn notified me this morning that the personnel I requested are already here," he said, pushing the up button for the elevator.

"Okay." Dani shifted Tessa, pressing a kiss to the infant's head.

The elevator doors opened, and they stepped out, Walsh leading into the Rock. Two men sat at the table with Skyler and Chance. Both wore black BDUs and navy blue short-sleeved T-shirts printed with the Nebraska State Patrol logo.

Knox trotted to Destiny. The shepherd glanced up from her place in the corner and they shared a customary sniffing. Graham, Elijah, Tiandra, and K-9 Bosco joined. The Malinois moved to join the other dogs. Walsh greeted the troopers then conducted introductions with his team.

The troopers got to their feet. The shorter of them, a husky man with a kind face and smiling eyes, stepped forward first. "Good morning. I'm Vernon Ulrich and this is John Nguyen."

"We met at the hospital, though not formally," Walsh replied with a glance at Nguyen. He offered handshakes to both. "I'm Commander Beckham

Walsh. Thank you for agreeing to help us with the protection detail."

"Glad to be of service," Trooper Nguyen said.

Dani introduced herself to the troopers as Walsh circled the room, sidling to the far side. Today, the action didn't appear as standoffish. Rather, he took the seat at the head of the table, as a leader should. She blinked, realizing how her biased perception had skewed her reality.

Eliana, K-9 Ammo, and Riker entered, quickly introducing themselves. Eliana sat beside her. The tension evaporated from Dani's body at the team's inclusion.

"I'm guessing this is our protection asset?" Trooper Ulrich said, making a silly face at the infant that earned him a giggle.

"This is Tessa," Dani said.

"Pleased to meet you, Ms. Tessa." Ulrich held out both hands, and she eagerly reached for him. Dani gently passed the infant to him. "I have three littles of my own at home," he told her.

"We're expecting our first," Nguyen said. "This will be great on-the-job training." He smiled.

"We plan to keep Tessa here, as it seems to be the most central and secure place for her," Walsh explained.

"We've set up an area," Eliana added. "There's a locker room, bunks and shower facilities as well."

"Follow me, and I'll show you around," Riker said.

They stepped out, with Ulrich entertaining Tessa with his silliness.

Walsh smiled, calling the group to order. "Troopers Ulrich and Nguyen will board here, taking shifts until we have a better handle on things."

"How long are you thinking?" Chance asked.

"Not sure." Walsh shot a glance at Dani. After a short debrief, Walsh advised the team of he and Dani's plans to visit Decorah and they departed from the group.

Dani contemplated stopping to see Tessa once more, then decided against it. The delay would only make it harder to leave the baby.

Dani and Walsh loaded into his SUV and got on the road. The drive was quiet and pleasant through Nebraska. When they reached the northeastern part of Iowa, acres of rolling hills surrounded them on the way to Decorah.

"We're about fifteen minutes out," Walsh advised.

"I'm not sure what I expect to find at the ice caves, but if Jayne kept that note, it has to mean something, right?" Dani asked.

"I agree. And as of now, we don't have any other leads, so I'd say we leave no ice cave unturned."

Dani chuckled at his combination of clichés, an endearing trait she'd forgotten that she loved about him. Loved? She studied him. Walsh's muscular form and handsome exterior hadn't faded with age.

But loved?

It was just a figure of speech. She shoved away the thought. It wasn't as though she had those feelings for Walsh. At least, not anymore.

Or did she? The days they'd spent together had

revealed the degrees that Walsh had matured since their younger romance. His steadfastness and support when she'd felt out of her depth only added to his handsome exterior features. She also couldn't deny that her heart did a triple beat and warmth radiated up her neck whenever he glanced at her.

"I appreciate everything you and your team have done to help Tessa and I." Dani deliberately left out Jayne's name to avoid ruining the peaceful moment. She didn't want to debate with Walsh today.

"As Tiandra said, it's what family does." Walsh never took his eyes off the road while simultaneously sipping his coffee.

"I'm sure the troopers will do a great job with her, though. We don't want to overstay our babysitting welcome."

"I don't think that's an issue."

Still, it was a temporary solution to a larger problem. Dani's responsibility for Tessa was becoming clearer by the minute. Jayne's condition continued to decline. They were on borrowed time before Dani would face the hardest decision of her life. Whether to establish permanent guardianship for Tessa.

Unwilling to deal with those thoughts today, she shoved them aside.

"Baby protection duty is highly unusual," Dani replied.

"I'd say most of our cases end up taking on that classification in one form or another."

"How so?"

"We've accumulated assets like Eliana's computer

technical skills and her DNA phenotyping program. Chance and Destiny are a force to be reckoned with as manhunt experts, and Elijah brings a wealth of street experience to our unit. Not to mention a shared face with Graham, so it works great for undercover ops."

Dani tried absorbing the information. "Yeah, I suppose you all are used to handling unique situations."

"Couldn't make this up if I wanted to." Walsh chuckled.

Dani relished the sound, enjoying the laugh lines that appeared around his brown eyes. "Your team also resembles the law enforcement version of *Love Connection.*"

"Tell me about it." He grinned, flicking a glance at her.

Their gazes held for several long seconds, transitioning into an awkward moment. Dani swallowed hard.

Walsh cleared his throat, then sipped his coffee. She averted her eyes, then shuffled with the contents of her purse. Dani couldn't deny the attraction building between them. She'd caught herself inhaling deeper to breathe in his aftershave.

When they'd driven a few miles, Dani said, "The task force's reputation precedes you. Even at Lincoln PD, I heard wonderful things about HFTF." She didn't add how the talk around the law enforcement community about Beckham Walsh's achievements poured salt in their estrangement wound. She'd struggled after Chief Varmose's debacle, while Walsh had soared in his career, promoting up the ranks. He'd fallen off her radar for a period, then reappeared when she learned of his return to the Marshals and subsequently advancing as the commander of HFTF.

Signposts advertised Palisades Park ahead, but construction signs near the entrance advised the area was closed to tourists.

"Why aren't there roadblocks restricting access?" Walsh asked, slowing to a stop.

"We might not be able to drive through, but can we walk in?" Dani offered. "Or perhaps what I should say is they won't see us sneaking through." She snickered.

"I'd say it's worth a try." Walsh parked the SUV as close as he could get to the entrance.

They unloaded and Dani leashed Knox. "Once more, Eliana to the rescue. She provided a backpack of hiking supplies."

"Remind me to give her a raise for her thoughtfulness," Walsh quipped.

Dani double-checked the items, and her heart swelled with appreciation for the tech's kindness. "No, you really need to. Eliana thought of everything down to bottled water." She zipped the pack closed and hoisted it onto her back.

"Ready?"

"Yep." They started up the trail. "For all the K-9s you have on the team, I'm surprised you're not a handler," she said. "You're a natural with them. Knox already adores you, and that's saying a lot. He doesn't take well to men in particular."

Walsh gave the dog a quick pat. "I wouldn't have thought that at all. He seems super at ease with me."

"That's what I mean. He's usually standoffish until he's decided whether the person has passed muster with him. But he acts like he's known you and your team members forever."

"I just extended the proverbial trust branch, and he accepted," Walsh agreed.

Dani grinned at his misuse of the cliché. "Guess animals sense when someone is safe." She considered the comment, realizing she truly believed it. If Knox trusted Walsh, then maybe she could as well. Except emotionally distancing herself by holding onto the past was the only thing that kept Dani from falling for Walsh.

Again. Once had cost her enough. She couldn't afford a second.

If only her heart agreed.

The brisk morning air had Dani tugging her jacket tighter.

Though it was a weekday, Dani expected other tourists hiking in the area. "Is it just me, or are we all alone out here?"

"I'd say you assessed it correctly."

Knox stopped to sniff at a tree before continuing.

They hiked through the woods to an ice cave sign that marked the tourist attraction further up the path.

Knox paused again, this time with his snout lifted.

"What's he saying?" Walsh asked.

"I'm not sure." Dani hesitated and studied her canine. "Knox, seek."

The dog stood still, actively sniffing the air.

"He's explosive detection trained, correct?" Walsh asked.

"This isn't his alert response." A chill passed over Dani as she surveyed their surroundings.

The path stretched out before them, bordered by trees heavily laden with leaves shadowing the dirt floor. A breeze fluttered, wafting the earthy, fresh scent of rain in the air. "Do you smell that?"

"It's called petrichor. Yeah, we'd better hurry this along if there's a storm headed our way."

Knox paused and barked, focused on a shadowed area. Walsh removed his gun. "Get to the side. I'll check it out."

They hadn't seen another driver the entire trip to the park. Had someone followed them? If so, how had the person gotten in without them noticing? She shifted away from the path, taking shelter behind a massive boulder.

Walsh and Knox disappeared around a bend. Only the chirrups of the birds overhead carried to her.

The snap of a twig to her right set Dani on edge and she froze. *Please Lord, help me to be silent and not make a sound.*

Her heart drummed hard against her chest in what felt like the longest minute of her life. *Where are you, Walsh?*

Finally, a dog's familiar paw clicking and boots stepping closer preceded Walsh and Knox's return. Dani exited her hiding spot and spotted Walsh's wide grin.

"Just a herd of deer," he announced.

"Knox doesn't get much exposure to those." Dani chuckled. "At the end of the day, he's still a dog." She gave the canine a good scratch behind the ears.

"The animals enthralled Knox, but to my surprise, he never barked at them," Walsh commended, kneeling to praise the canine.

They continued the ascent to the ice cave high above the town of Decorah. Stone steps and a majestic rock formation towered overhead, revealing the entrance. The floor disappeared into the cavernous core.

The temperature dropped dramatically as they ventured further into the cavern. Walsh removed a flashlight from his cargo pants' pocket and swept the beam into the dark depths.

"What exactly are we looking for?" Dani's voice reverberated in the confined space. She tugged Knox closer beside her.

"Wish I knew," Walsh said.

The path grew narrower.

"Good thing I'm not claustrophobic," Dani half joked.

Knox stuck his snout into a crevice, backed up, then gently descended into a sphinx pose.

Dani froze. "Don't move."

"What's wrong?" Walsh turned, illuminating Knox with the flashlight beam.

"Knox, seek," Dani commanded.

The K-9 rose slowly, again nudged his nose into the fissure and backed up, returning to the sphinx pose.

Dani spun to look at the path from where they'd

come. A thin stream of sunlight illuminated the entrance behind them.

Too far away.

"Knox is alerting to explosives."

"We have to get out of here!"

Dani took the lead, and they started to retrace their steps toward the exit.

An earsplitting explosion showered them with falling rocks.

Dani squatted, Walsh ducked beside her, shielding Dani and Knox with his massive frame.

Before she caught her breath, a second blast in front of them collapsed the cave entrance, thrusting them into darkness.

Walsh's ears rang, and the piercing sound dragged him into the depths of his memories. He returned to the Middle East, surrounded by gunfire and IEDs blasting in every direction. The desperate shouts of his comrades screaming orders and warnings.

Walsh gasped, hands stretched outward to ground himself. Anticipating the familiar grit of sand, he startled at the soft fur in his grasp.

Like a lifeline, he clung to the dog and allowed the sensation to stabilize him. The warmth of his coat under Walsh's fingers and the animal's rhythmic panting calmed him. His mind worked to sort between the past and present, filtering the atmosphere and smells. Memories of the endless days in the desert during his deployments overseas.

"Walsh."

Dani.

This wasn't Afghanistan.

He was in Iowa.

Sitting in a cave.

*Be present.* The silent command soothed him, and muscle memory kicked in. Walsh began combat breathing. *Inhale. Hold. Count to four. Exhale. Hold. Count to four.*

"Walsh! Are you hurt? Where are you?" Dani's voice reached to him like a beacon.

He blinked, realizing his eyes were wide open yet the darkness encroached on him in all directions. "Dani."

"Yes! Are you and Knox okay?" she repeated.

"We're fine. I think." Walsh tasted the dirt and grit. A wet swipe across his cheek made Walsh laugh. "Thanks, Knox."

"What did he do?" Dani asked, voice trembling.

"Offered reassurance." Walsh shifted. Pain radiated from his thigh, and he sucked in a breath. He winced, gently probing the area. Blood. He'd may have spoken too soon. "I'm guessing we found some of those missing military explosives," he said dryly, cringing at the badly timed joke.

"Unfortunately, I think you're right," Dani said.

Walsh slapped at the ground, grasping the flashlight beside his leg and pressed the button. Nothing happened. His fingers brushed the shattered lens. "Great."

"What's wrong?"

"I dropped the flashlight in the blast and broke it."

"Use your cell phone app," Dani suggested.

Impressed by her calmness, Walsh withdrew the device and activated the app, casting a soft glow into the space. Dust clouds filled the air as the rocks settled. At first glance, the area to the entrance was blocked by avalanched stone. Panic seized his chest, and he shoved it down, shifting into command mode. He got to his feet, gritting his teeth against the pain searing his thigh.

"Whoa! What happened?" Dani exclaimed, hurrying toward the light.

He glanced down at the shale piercing his leg. She leaned over, inspecting the injury. "Hold on. It's a puncture, but nowhere near the femoral artery. I'll pull it out." Dani eased off the backpack and withdrew an extra T-shirt Eliana must've packed. She really thought of everything.

"All right. Don't tell me when—"

Dani yanked out the piece and Walsh howled, biting back words his mother wouldn't have approved. She pressed the fabric hard against the wound. "Hold that."

Walsh did as she instructed, and within seconds, she'd fashioned a tourniquet and bandage. Her touch was strong and exhilarating.

The bulletproof vest he wore did nothing to protect his heart from the radical arrhythmia being around Dani inflicted. Walsh returned to combat breathing while focusing on the plan of escape. Anything to stop the dangerous thoughts his mind wanted him to venture into.

"Are you in a lot of pain?" Dani asked, her face too close to his. The floral scent of her hair wafted to him above the dusty air.

"I'm fine," he replied, avoiding the real question. He pushed back and, using the stone wall, got to his feet. "Stay here. I'll look for a way out of here."

Unable to see Dani in the ambient glow, Walsh moved to the crumbled rocks and spotted a sliver of sunlight. With all his strength, he pushed at the boulder. His leg raged in pain, draining his energy, but Walsh refused to surrender. He'd faced worse in prior missions. He repositioned, and after several unsuccessful attempts, shoved the massive rock aside, creating a gap. "It's a tight space, but big enough to wiggle through." At least Dani and Knox would. And they could bring back help if Walsh couldn't get through.

Dani approached. "That won't be large enough for us."

"Not for me, but you and Knox will fit," he replied.

"Negative." Dani motioned for him to hand her the phone.

He smirked, passing her the device. Using the flashlight beam, she inspected the area.

"Here, if you can move this rock, too, it'll give us space to get out."

Walsh did as she instructed, and the stack shifted. His heart stuttered. Would it collapse and trap them permanently? Finally, the shaking subsided. True to Dani's assessment, the change created a wide opening for them to squeeze through.

"Ladies first," Walsh said.

Dani eased through and Knox followed, making the escape look easy. Walsh sucked in his breath and partially inched into the tight fit. Then he stopped.

"What's wrong?" Dani asked.

"Nothing beyond a good diet and no more donuts," he grunted, pressing all his weight back against the stones. At last, he freed himself from the collapsed section.

But the getaway wasn't over.

Fallen rock and cave formations littered the ground, creating an obstacle course in the confined space. Aiming for the splintering sunlight, they exited in a rush, but remained within the tall stone walls surrounding it.

Walsh surveyed the area. Remnants of the explosives the bomber had used fluttered near the entrance.

"Was this an accidental explosion of the stolen/hidden munitions we happened upon at the right time and place, or was it a deliberate attempt to kill us?" Dani asked.

"No clue," Walsh grumbled. "Neither is acceptable." Except they'd either discovered the stash of missing evidence, now destroyed…or the other option meant they remained in danger.

Dani voiced his next thoughts. "If it was an attacker, do you think he stuck around?"

"Let me check first," Walsh said.

Once they stepped away from the cave, they were exposed to whoever waited for them. He inched from the stone formations, peering into the park. "I don't see anyone." Walsh took the lead, with Dani following.

They retraced their way on the hiking path. His leg throbbed, but he didn't complain.

The birds chirping cheerfully overhead were oblivious to the nearly devastating demise Walsh and Dani had just endured.

Both remained silent, with only their footfalls on the gravel as background noise.

The sight of the SUV brought immense relief until they drew closer.

Fury fueled Walsh's steps. The pain in his leg forgotten considering the vehicle's slashed tires. "You have got to be kidding me!"

He started to storm forward, instantly restricted by Dani's arm holding him back. "Let Knox check just in case there's an unwanted explosive in this SUV too."

"Good idea."

Dani knelt beside the K-9 and removed his leash. "Knox. Search."

His stumpy tail wagged in response, and Dani repeated the order. "Knox. Search!"

The Dobie mix went into work mode, sniffing the vehicle's perimeter. He made no indications before returning to Dani's side.

"He says it's clear," she interpreted.

A short measure of relief coursed through Walsh. "At least the bomber spared this SUV," he mumbled sarcastically. After calling 9-1-1 to report the incident, he said, "Help is on the way, but we're stuck until they arrive."

He popped the trunk, and they sat on the deck while he called the task force. Walsh set his phone between them, activating the speakerphone so Dani could interact as well.

Eliana answered the office line. "Heartland Fugitive—"

"We found some of the missing evidence and almost died. Again," Walsh barked.

"Sir?" Eliana inquired.

"Someone blew up the ice cave or we happened upon live munitions that accidentally went off while we were searching," Walsh said. "Either way, it nearly killed us."

Eliana gasped. "Are you okay?"

"Yes, we're fine."

"Walsh has a laceration on his left leg," Dani reported.

Why did she have to go telling them that? "No big deal."

Thankfully, Eliana didn't press the issue. "If it was an attack, how did the person know you were out there?"

"My question exactly," Walsh grumbled. "We'll be in touch after we've spoken with the responders. In the meantime, advise the team it's probable the bomber used part of the missing evidence in the cave. If it was coincidental, there could be more live munitions in there."

"Will do," Eliana said, disconnecting.

"You gotta learn to say 'hello' before starting a conversation," Dani said. Her tone was half teasing and though she tried to smile, it never fully reached her eyes.

"I keep hearing that. I focus on the goal and forget to be polite. Comes from years of barking orders." Again, his mind drifted back to his military service.

"To cops?"

"Yes, but first in the marines."

"You served? I never knew that."

"Joined after the Varmose investigation. I was the OIC Marine in the Middle East. Pleasantries aren't an option when you're constantly dodging danger."

"You were an officer in charge." Dani's expression sobered. "Wow. You're right. My bad."

And this wasn't the time to have this conversation. It would inevitably lead to other personal discussions like that of his widower status. Thankfully, his phone chimed with a text. He glanced down and read Eliana's message aloud for Dani. "'BOLO for Aiden De-Luca revealed a burned-up truck in the middle of a cornfield outside of Fremont.'"

"That's concerning."

"Yeah."

"Were there indicators of victims inside the vehicle?" Dani asked.

"No, it was empty," Walsh confirmed as he continued to read. He shook his head, responding to the message with a thumbs-up emoji, then pocketing the phone.

"Attempt to hide evidence?"

"Possibly." Walsh slid off the tailgate and leaned against the SUV.

Dani removed the backpack and withdrew two bottled waters, passing one to Walsh. "We could've died back there."

"But we didn't," Walsh reminded her.

"I cannot make careless decisions like that. If something happens to me, and Jayne doesn't recover…" Dani's voice cracked on the last word. She paused, then continued, "Who would take care of Tessa?" Her soft tone carried self-condemnation.

Walsh looked down, kicking at the dirt. "Dani, this isn't on you. I should've brought in reinforcements."

"You can't send a ten-person team to follow every lead," Dani argued. "A mother's intuition would've probably kicked in before entering the cave. Jayne wouldn't have acted that foolishly."

She was hard on herself. "But you're not Tessa's mother," Walsh replied. At the hurt that flashed over Dani's expression, he instantly regretted his comment. What had he said wrong? He'd meant to comfort her and instead he'd alienated her.

Attempting to right the offense, he said, "Tessa is safe at the Rock, which proves you were looking out for her best interest. She's with caregivers who have the time and capability for a consistent schedule too," Walsh said, trying to make the situation better.

"Understood." Dani's flattened lips and posture implied his efforts had made things worse. "Our jobs are high risk."

"Yes. So, let's take down this criminal for good." *Stop talking!* He was shoveling the hole deeper for himself.

"Right. Parenting belongs to those designed for it, which is why I've never become one," Dani snapped. "Taking down criminals is what I'm built for." Her declaration didn't match her stance. "Rather than drive back to Grand Island, I'd like to stay at the task force condo, if that's acceptable."

"Sure."

But a plan bloomed in Walsh's mind, and he grinned.

Sirens wailed, growing louder and interrupting the discussion.

He turned as strobing lights approached. "I'll handle the report."

They were going somewhere safe. Together.

# ELEVEN

By the time they were finally on the road again, heading west to Nebraska, exhaustion overwhelmed Dani. Walsh's comment at the cave annoyed her with the itch of a mosquito bite. Consistency? How was she supposed to do that with a maniac determined to kill her? More so, she hated that she completely agreed with him.

She wasn't mom material, not in her current role. Sure, she could care for Tessa and provide for her basic necessities, but mothers had to have more than that ability. A mother needed to be available for her child. Dani's responsibilities and work hours interfered with that. She couldn't guarantee when she'd be home. She hesitated, her emotions whirling. Was she selfish to consider balancing her career and parenting?

The words tumbled in her brain, tormenting her. They'd nearly died.

And it confirmed the truth that she'd always believed. The challenges of child-rearing and giving one hundred percent to her high-intensity job didn't mix. She'd experienced that growing up with a constantly worn-out single mother. She'd tried to be enough for everyone and never met the mark. Too often Dani suffered as her mother's career took precedence over their schedule. She'd never complained. If she'd been less of a burden, her father wouldn't have traded Dani and Mom in for another family. She'd never do anything to make her mom abandon her too.

But her child heart had missed her mother. The all-too-often times Dani had spent with a sitter or by herself had erected protective walls mortared by vows to never put anyone through that sorrow.

"In light of the attempts on our lives," Walsh said, interrupting her contemplations, "it's imperative we find a safe place to reevaluate this case. If the attacker is pursuing us, returning to the Rock draws attention to where Tessa is."

"I agree."

"Great. What're your views on staying with Marissa?"

"Your sister?" she asked incredulously. "Would she want that?"

"I took the liberty of asking her before proposing the idea to you." He lifted a hand in surrender. "Just in case. Marissa readily agreed on the assignment."

Dani contemplated the option. They had been friends years ago, but they'd lost touch. She knew nothing about Marissa's current life. As though sensing her hesitation, Walsh said, "If you're not comfortable with it, we'll come up with something else."

"No, it's not that." Dani measured her next words, not wanting to offend him. "It's just… We've had multiple attempts on our lives. You'd never forgive me if your only sister was hurt."

Walsh flicked a glance at her, meeting her eyes for several seconds before returning his attention to the road. "Marissa's tougher than you think. She was a marine before her recent retirement."

"Are we talking about the same person?" Dani asked, picturing the petite, soft-spoken woman who didn't fit the criteria of a hard-core military officer.

"Yep," he replied. "She's one tough brownie."

Dani grinned again at his misuse of the idiom. "Well, that puts a whole different spin on things."

"While assisting HFTF on another investigation, Marissa was almost killed," Walsh said.

"What?" Dani gasped. "When? How?"

"Long story. Suffice it to say, she came out stronger than ever and she's undeterred by fear."

Dani swallowed hard, humbled by the information. "Then, yes, I'd love to visit with Marissa and work on the case."

"Excellent."

She glanced at the backseat where Tessa's car seat would've been and sighed. "Are we meeting Marissa in Omaha?"

"Actually, I figured we'd go to our horse ranch in Ponca and set up a temporary BOO there."

"You want to make your place the base of operations for this case?" Dani clarified.

"Won't be the first time."

"Fine with me." She shrugged. "But we're covering serious miles."

"Get some rest," Walsh said. "I'll wake you when we arrive."

"No need to ask me twice." Dani leaned back and

closed her eyes, dreaming of Tessa's sweet face and laughter.

Before she realized it, Walsh's voice drew her out of her peaceful sleep. "Dani."

She inched upward in her seat, stunned the sun was setting low in the sky. "How long was I out?"

"The remaining three hours of the drive." He smiled kindly. "But you needed it, besides Knox kept me company with his snoring as entertainment." He jerked his chin slightly toward the back.

Dani twisted around, spotting her dog stretched out on the seat. He sighed and yawned. "Good boy, Knox."

She surveyed the landscape as Walsh pulled onto a private lane surrounded by lush green rolling hills. Thick cottonwoods canopied overhead, and a split-rail fence bordered the acreage. He drove under an archway, suspended by log posts, sporting a sign that read Meadowlark Lane Ranch in black wrought-iron letters.

"This is yours?" Dani didn't bother disguising her awe.

"Well, me and Marissa. We share the property, though she maintains it full-time while working with our horses." Pride filled Walsh's tone.

He pulled up to a ranch-style house constructed of gray siding, stone accents and white trim. An inviting wraparound porch overshadowed the barn doors in front of the walkout basement. A variety of horses meandered behind the fence.

Walsh shut off the engine and Dani released Knox.

"Becky! You made it!"

Dani turned to see Marissa hurrying down the house steps toward them. She threw herself into Walsh's arms for a bear hug.

"I love that you still call him Becky." Dani circled the vehicle.

"Yeah, it's a treat," he groaned with a smile.

Marissa chuckled. "My favorite nickname for him because he hates it. It's great to see you!" She rushed to Dani and pulled her into a tight embrace. "You haven't aged a single day! Tell me how."

Dani felt her cheeks warm. "Flattery will get you everywhere. You look amazing!"

"It's the good life, living in bliss with them." Marissa gestured at the majestic horses. The animals had strolled closer to the fence, curious about the newcomers.

Dani smiled. "I can't wait to meet them all."

Marissa leaned down. "Come on in. Let's get you settled. I made dinner too."

"Best. Sister. Ever," Walsh replied.

"Tell me something I don't already know," Marissa teased. "Hey, Becky, maybe put your vehicle in the Morton building?"

"Good idea."

Dani reached for Knox's leash while Walsh slid behind the wheel and backed away from the house. She trailed Marissa up the steps and into the home. If the exterior had awed Dani, the interior dumbfounded her.

The welcoming open concept home had a stone

fireplace centered in the living room, opposite a kitchen and dining area. Delicious aromas wafted to them, and hunger assailed Dani for the first time since the nightmare had begun.

Marissa led her down a hallway and gestured to a large bedroom with a queen bed.

Touched by her thoughtfulness, Dani settled onto the bed, realizing she had no clothes or personal supplies. She'd not intended for the Decorah trip to extend to overnights in Ponca. As though sensing her worry, Marissa said, "I stocked the bathroom with essentials, and there are clothes in the closet and dresser drawers."

"You thought of everything."

"Hopefully. Sounds like you all have been through the wringer." Marissa paused. "C'mon, Zink, out from under the bed."

Dani tilted her head, unsure what she was talking about. An orange flash of fur darted past Knox and out to the hallway. Knox turned and barked. "No!" Dani ordered. The dog whined but stayed in place. "Sorry, he's not used to being around cats. He won't hurt the kitty though."

"No worries. Zink can handle himself." Marissa winked. The sound of a door closed, and Knox woofed again. "Guess Becky's back. Let's go eat."

"Smells delicious." Dani stood. "I just need a minute to wash up, and I'll be right there."

"Sounds good. Make yourself at home." Marissa exited the room.

Thoughts of Tessa made Dani's heart squeeze. She

missed the baby. "Take care of her, Lord," she prayed aloud.

As much as Dani had justified to Walsh why she couldn't or shouldn't be a mother to Tessa, she wondered if parenting was still a possibility. But if that happened, how would she explain to Tessa that her mother was dead because of Dani's failure to protect her?

Tessa would hate her.

Dani wouldn't blame her.

Morning arrived too soon, but Walsh didn't want to waste time sleeping when he needed to be working on the case. He and Marissa were both up before sunrise, and she'd already gone outside to work with the horses. He sat at the dining table, watching through the window, and sipping her thick-as-oil coffee.

Dani hadn't emerged from her bedroom. She was probably still asleep, and that brought great relief to him. At least they'd rested without further attacks. He pushed back from the table and strolled closer to the window. In the pasture, Marissa rode Royal. The beautiful thoroughbred galloped with incredible grace. He was their first rescue. His previous owners had abandoned him in a kill pen after they'd gotten all they wanted from him. Clueless idiots who'd failed to see the majestic creature had so much life left in him. Fond memories of their dad's gentle but strong instruction on equine care returned to Walsh. Their parents had been deceased a long time, but he'd never stopped missing them.

Royal's pedigreed status hadn't changed, regardless of his age. His identity remained the same. Walsh paused, considering the similarities. Had he placed too much on his role as a marshal and not on his value as a person?

Walsh walked outside and leaned on the fence, watching his sister ride. Her thick auburn hair bounced around her shoulders. A grin spread across her lips when she saw him, and she trotted in his direction. Royal's hoofs pounded a staccato rhythm against the soft ground. When they reached him, Marissa pulled back on the reins and slid off the animal. She rubbed his neck. "Good job, Royal!"

The horse whinnied his appreciation.

"Feel like riding?" Marissa approached him.

"I would, but my mind is all over the place."

"That's when processing your musings is most productive." Marissa climbed up the fence and perched on the top rail.

"You only do that so you can look down on me," Walsh teased.

"So." She stuck out her tongue playfully. At six-foot-four-inches tall, Walsh towered over his five-foot-two baby sister. "How're you doing with the unexpected reunion?" Walsh flicked his gaze to Marissa, and she waved him off. "Don't even deny it. I can always read you, big brother."

"It's weird." He sighed. "At times, the guilt over Varmose's case hits me with terrible force. But when I look at Dani, I can't help wondering what could've been." His confession brought a release he'd not expected. Telling Marissa about his confusing feelings helped. That was something he could never do with his team as their commander.

"I figured Tessa might also trigger some of those old emotions."

"It does. Reminds me how I failed Gwen and lost any chance of having a family. I try to keep a distance, but she's a sweet baby." He frowned, kicking at a rock. "We're dodging a bomber, and I'm doing a lousy job of protecting Tessa and Dani."

"Are you sure Dani wants your protection?" Marissa asked. "Seems to me she's more than capable."

"Except whenever I enter the picture, I ruin everything for her." He shoved his hands into his jeans' pockets. "I've got a propensity to sweep the carpet out from underneath her."

Marissa chuckled. "First, it's a rug, not a carpet."

"Whatever." He swatted playfully at her.

"Second, Becky, you did your job taking down Varmose. He was corrupt. Telling Dani you were conducting an internal affairs investigation would've compromised your career and your case. She understands that. Especially now as a police chief."

"Does she?"

Marissa tilted her head. "Did she say otherwise?"

"Not specifically." Walsh reconsidered their conversations regarding Varmose. "I don't regret arresting that jerk. I can't stand anyone who abuses the badge. But I should've warned her. To protect Dani."

"You were a young detective. You made decisions with the information you had at that time. But I concur one hundred percent about Varmose abusing his position." Marissa sighed. "That's ancient history. Is that what's really bugging you?"

"Yes and no. It's playing into this whole mess. I can't stand that someone is trying to hurt her, and I can't stop it." *It adds to my inadequacies as a protector.* "I messed up and didn't shield her then, and I'm doing the same thing now," he confessed. "Multiple attacks from an assassin, her department's declining view of her, and the fallout from this case is too much." Walsh glanced down, remembering the way the GIPD personnel had spoken about Dani. "Not to mention, her stubbornness about Jayne is a replay of Varmose. She's got no one else, just like Tessa. I want to make all the bad go away for them both." And his heart's cry for a second chance with Dani beckoned for his attention.

"And…"

"Being around the baby with the retirement clock ticking is giving me a cruel reminder of what I never had. Remembering dreams Gwen and I lost."

"That's understandable." Marissa glanced past him at Royal, still trotting happily nearby. "But Gwen's situation was out of your hands."

"Was it? I didn't have to stay gone. I was busy chasing my ambitions, climbing the military ladder. Just like my goal in taking down Varmose clouded my judgment." He leaned with his back against the fence, facing the pond in the distance. "Seems my aspirations have done more damage than good. I should've come home when I knew Gwen was struggling."

"And if you had, would your presence alone have given her the will to live?"

At his sister's words, he turned.

Marissa's cerulean eyes bore into him. "Gwen ended her life. You didn't do it to her, nor were you the reason."

He snorted. "Right, tell that to her family."

"You're not responsible for their reactions, either," Marissa replied. "They were hurting, and people lash out when their emotions are super raw. You're allowed to keep living."

"I don't blame them." He paced a path in front of her. "Even if I could move on, how would I get past the memories of Gwen and the emotional tsunami attack her family brought down on me? Honestly, they're probably right that it's a good thing I never got to be a father. I was a lousy husband."

"You were serving your country, Becky." Marissa hopped down, standing in his way. "You cannot be on the battlefield facing real enemies with your mind on your troubled wife. There's no shame in that."

"Except I wasn't there for Gwen when she needed me, and then it was too late. And now my career is ending soon, and what do I have to show for it?" Walsh shook his head. "I'll be living out here talking to horses in my old age."

Marissa laughed. "Well, you won't be alone. I'll be right here with you."

"No way, you're still young and will have a life beyond this." He gestured toward the open spaces.

"So could you."

"Nope, it's too late."

"Wow, are you also stressing about world peace and global warming?" Marissa's eyes twinkled.

"Whatever." He swatted at her again.

"You're a powerful man, Beckham Walsh, but you are not in control of the universe. Past, present, or future. You certainly aren't the regulator of Gwen, Dani, or Tessa's futures. You can't keep trying to protect them right out of the Will of God."

His head whipped up. "What's that supposed to mean?"

"You're no one's savior. That responsibility belongs to God alone. You didn't kill Gwen. As awful and tragic as her death was for all of us, it's not yours to bear."

Walsh looked down.

"In respect to Dani, sometimes God uses the pain and hardships in our lives to mold us," Marissa said. "You want to keep running interference, so Dani and Tessa have no problems. Have you considered that God is using those things to strengthen them and build their character?"

He gaped at her. "You're suggesting I leave them exposed to a killer?"

"Of course not." She cuffed his shoulder. "Protection detail is part of your job. The only way to truly do that is to identify this mysterious shooter/bomber/assassin after you all. But that's not the protection you're talking about."

"Ugh, I hate that you know me so well." Walsh

scrubbed a hand over his head. "Dani hates me for not telling her about Varmose."

"Talk to her about it. She's not just a cop, Becky! Dani's the chief of police. She'll understand the position you faced." Marissa tugged at his sleeve. "And while you're at it, tell her how you've never stopped loving her."

Walsh blinked. "What? When did I ever say that?"

Marissa grinned conspiratorially. "She's standing at the window. Let's eat breakfast."

"Go on." Walsh's heart drummed hard against his chest. "I gotta ponder all this."

"Chicken." Marissa strolled past him toward the house.

He wandered the lane to the pond. Had he brought Dani here to cocoon her? If he had, was that wrong? It was his job to protect others.

But Marissa's comments lingered.

He walked to the small dock, studying the mirror-still water. Gwen had died twenty-two years ago. He didn't deserve to be happy. Wasn't that what her family had said to him at the funeral? And he'd accepted those words as his fate.

Yet Dani's return, looking more beautiful than she had when they'd dated thirty years ago, had awakened his heart. Marissa was dead on, Dani had demonstrated how much stronger she was now than when she'd worked for Varmose.

He'd heard rumors that she'd left the department after the chief's arrest and had figured she hadn't wanted to be tied to the corrupt behavior. Who could blame her? Dani exuded fortitude and confidence far beyond what he'd imagined she would. They'd faced a bomber/assassin while caring for Tessa. No effortless task. And she'd done it well. Had those earlier trials helped her to deal with today?

Walsh bowed his head, offering a prayer for wisdom and confessing his doubts and fears. He concluded it with the most terrifying words he'd ever spoken.

"Lord, use me how You deem fit. Regardless of the outcome."

# TWELVE

Dani settled into a chair.

"Hope you're hungry." Marissa placed plates of fruit, eggs, bacon, and potatoes in the center of the dining table. "I never have the privilege of cooking for others, so I might've overdone it a bit."

Dani laughed. "As long as you promise not to tell anyone when I stuff myself."

Marissa smirked. "No problem. Coffee?"

"I'll get it." Dani walked to the brewer, snagging a mug on the way. "Is Walsh joining us?"

"When he's done wandering the grounds."

Dani stifled her disappointment, baffled why she cared. That wasn't true. She'd looked forward to seeing him first thing this morning. Being around him was comfortable, and it all felt right.

Marissa sat opposite her. "How're you holding up?"

"Last night was a reprieve. I feel like a new person." She spooned food onto her plate.

"I hear that."

Dani hadn't missed the way Walsh had averted his gaze when he'd caught her looking out the window before walking away from the house. Biting into the bacon, she teased, "Is it bad if there's nothing left for him?"

"Nope. You snooze, you lose."

"I'm glad to see you didn't get your brother's cliché confusion problem."

Marissa laughed. "He's a hoot." She leaned back in her seat, both hands cradling her coffee mug. "Becky's pouting because I scolded him."

"Really, about what?" At Marissa's pause, Dani said, "Sorry. I'm nosy."

"I reminded him his macho save-the-world complex was unnecessary."

"Comes with the job, I suppose."

"Partially. Mostly, it's guilt for not being the ultimate protector." Marissa sipped her coffee. "Becky keeps that grudge alive by nursing it."

A twinge of conscience nudged Dani. "We stopped talking after he arrested my Cortez PD chief. You already know that."

"Some."

Dani longed to avoid the conversation. Out of respect for Marissa, she forced herself to remain seated. "Varmose's corruption tanked his career and landed him in jail. Imagine my surprise when I learned the person I trusted was a criminal behind a badge."

"No kidding."

"That wasn't the worst. When my coworkers discovered Walsh and I were dating, they turned their hatred at me, assuming I was involved in the sting."

"No." Marissa leaned forward. "Dani! What did you do?"

"They made my life miserable. When I couldn't take any more, I quit." She grabbed a grape. "The Cortez PD hate squad tried bad-mouthing me to other agencies as a backstabber. Thankfully, their tactics didn't work. News spreads fast among law enforcement, and Varmose's nefarious activities didn't involve me, which helped my situation. I worked in smaller towns before Lincoln PD hired me."

"Is Becky aware of this?"

Dani shrugged, absently pushing food around her plate. "Anyone within a forty-mile radius would've heard."

"That explains it. Becky joined the military after the takedown. He blamed himself for not telling you in advance."

Dani sat straighter. "Why didn't he warn me?"

"He understood your position and propensity to be loyal—"

"To a fault."

"Exactly. If he'd told you, you'd notify Varmose, jeopardize the case, and Walsh's career." Marissa sipped her coffee. "Ironically, he resigned from the agency, anyway."

"Wow." Dani sighed. "He's right. I would've told Varmose, because I stupidly believed in his innocence...until I saw the evidence and he openly confessed." She shook her head. "If I was in Walsh's shoes, I would've done the same."

"That introduction into IAs took a toll on him." Marissa referenced internal affairs investigations. "That was his first and last one. You're nobody's friend when you're the cop working cases involving other cops."

Dani hadn't considered Walsh's sacrifice. Ultimately, doing the right thing at an extreme price.

"He relocated to North Carolina, met and married Gwen, then deployed overseas soon after."

That got Dani's attention. "Walsh was married?" Did the comment sound as jealous as the words tasted?

"He's never told you about Gwen?"

"No." Dani's chest tightened at the woman's name and accompanying unfamiliar emotion. Jealousy.

Marissa sighed. "Their relationship was tough from the start. Gwen hated the marines kept him gone for long stretches of time. She constantly pleaded for him to return stateside. He used up his leave trying to appease her, but it's the military. You can't turn in a sick day request in the middle of a war." Marissa forked potatoes, and Dani eagerly waited for her to continue. "Gwen struggled with mental illness and refused to seek help. She took her own life while Becky was deployed."

Dani gasped, putting a hand over her mouth. Her throat tightened. She'd put her anger and disdain on Walsh when he'd already suffered so much. Her heart ached for him. "Poor Walsh!"

"Yep. Then her family tore after Becky with a vengeance. Tried making his life miserable. They blamed him and said a better husband would've helped his wife. Which, of course, is a lie. Walsh did all he could."

Dani sat dumbfounded. She'd misjudged Walsh. As though sensing her shift in emotions, Knox nudged her hand and laid his head in her lap. "Hey, sweetie."

"He's in tune with you."

"Honestly, Knox is a great comfort dog." She stroked his short fur.

"Nothing wrong with that," Marissa said.

"Maybe someday I'll train those types of dogs." Dani paused. Where had that thought come from? "I didn't mean to interrupt what you were saying. Please, go on."

Marissa finished swallowing. "Gwen's family tormented Becky. Contacting him with reminders of her and dishing out guilt. They said he didn't deserve happiness."

"That's ludicrous. It wasn't his fault!"

"Becky accepted the lies." Marissa shrugged. "He never dated again. That's why he's a hopeless workaholic."

"I never knew." Dani picked at a strawberry on her plate. "He processed his grief by avoidance."

"Basically."

"Anybody would understand his position. Besides, a man's emotional wounds endears him to women," Dani thought aloud. "A woman's repels men." Thus, why she'd maintained her relationship paralysis.

"Not sure I agree," Marissa contended. "Careers like the military and law enforcement encourage the façade of impenetrable strength. Nobody goes through life unscathed by pain or disappointment. There's nothing wrong with admitting where we are, but sometimes people assume vulnerability and humility are synonymous."

"One feeds the other?"

"No." Marissa shook her head. "Humility isn't weakness, it's recognizing our deepest need for God."

Dani considered the words. "How long ago did all this happen with Gwen?"

"Over twenty years," Marissa said. "There's a lot Becky should've shared with you."

"Maybe if I'd given him a safe place to talk, he would've."

"Been hard on him?" Marissa asked with the confidence of someone already familiar with the answer.

"Yeah. I owe him an apology." Dani looked up.

Walsh leaned against the kitchen entrance.

"Perfect opportunity," Marissa whispered. "I need to check on the horses." She rushed out of the room.

"You overheard us?" Dani asked.

"Yes." Walsh crossed to the sink and washed his hands before sliding into a chair beside her. "She shouldn't have told you all that."

"I'm glad she did." Dani met his gaze. Compassion swelled for the man who'd tried to do the right thing many times, only to be hurt. "I'm sorry for the pain you've endured."

Defeat seemed to press on his shoulders. "I brought it on myself."

"No, you didn't." The condemnation she'd held against him vanished. There was so much more to Beckham Walsh than she'd realized. Before Dani realized it, she blurted, "My ex-husband claimed he didn't want children. He pretended to support my career pursuits, then later walked out on me for another woman with whom he built a family." Dani stared at her fork.

"Wow." Walsh touched her hand, quickly withdrawing. "Did you want children?"

Dani shrugged. "I suppose some women do. I saw the way my mom struggled as a working parent and didn't think I could do it."

Walsh didn't comment as he piled a plate high with eggs and bacon. A piece of meat landed on the floor, and he leaned down to grab it. Knox rushed over, snatching the treat. "Beat me to it." He laughed and sat up.

"Sorry about that. He's well-trained, but he's still a dog." Dani met his gaze, grateful for the interruption. She caught a glimpse of yellow stuck to his forehead and stifled a grin.

"What?"

"You must've brushed your head on your plate." She leaned closer, and using a napkin, wiped away the scrambled egg. "You had a little egg on your face."

He grinned. "That seems to happen a lot lately."

Dani smiled, not moving. She'd forgotten how handsome he was when she wasn't looking at him through eyes of disdain and blame. "Thank you for sharing your past with me."

He tilted his head. "In all fairness, my sister did that."

Their gaze lingered. Her breath quickened and Dani inched closer, inhaling his aftershave. She lifted her chin.

The doorbell rang, and Knox barked and hurried

to the door. The combination had Walsh and Dani flinging backward in their seats.

Her focus reverted to her dog. Had he saved her from making a huge mistake or interrupted something wonderful?

"I'll be right back." Walsh excused himself.

Dani fixed her gaze on her breakfast. "I need to remind myself where I am," she mumbled.

In the middle of a case where her friend might die, orphan her daughter, or end up incarcerated. The outlandishness of the moment hit Dani. She'd become the one Jayne would blame.

Just as Dani had done to Walsh.

Ironic.

Knox waited for Walsh. The dog had saved him from making a huge mistake. Dani knew about Gwen. No woman wanted a man who'd failed to protect his ill wife. With a sigh, he tugged open the door.

Riker and his Dutch shepherd, Ammo, stood on the other side.

A perfectly timed visual reminder of his responsibilities.

"Dani's in danger," Riker whispered.

Walsh stepped outside, closing the door. They sat in the chairs on the front porch.

"That's already established," Walsh grunted, stretching out his legs.

"No, more so. Eliana located intel on the dark web that someone put a hit out on Dani."

"What?" Walsh bellowed and then lowered his voice. "Drill deeper and find out who!"

"She's trying, but it's difficult. The creep covered his tracks." Riker leaned against the railing. Ammo laid down with a sigh.

Walsh sat forward, elbows on his knees.

"Are you holding up okay, boss?"

He appreciated the concern, but a leader didn't have the luxury of falling apart in front of his team. "As well as expected." He scrubbed his palm over his face. "We need a lead, and fast."

Riker, like the rest of the task force, understood that once a case went cold, it took substantial reviving to keep it active.

"We're working nonstop."

Walsh exhaled a deep breath. "HFTF is the best. We'll solve this. I just abhor the in-between time."

A cardinal sang overhead, and the crisp morning air held a scent of lilacs, reminding Walsh how he loved this place. In the distance, several horses meandered in the east pasture.

"Sir, all due respect—"

"I hate that phrase," Walsh grumbled good-naturedly.

Riker chuckled, sitting in the chair beside him. "Jayne Bardot's guilty for the missing evidence. Only her motive is questionable. With or without Aiden, she's the strongest connection. We're wasting time looking for something that's right in front of our faces. Dani's trying to defend her, but everything points to Jayne and Aiden as cohorts. Why aren't we pressing charges instead of stalling based on her surmised innocence?"

"I hope your team didn't assume that about you when someone framed you for murder," Dani said.

Walsh and Riker twisted around to see Dani standing beside the open window. She shifted, opening the door. "All I've asked is that we don't make assumptions without fully investigating this case."

Riker looked down, and Walsh's neck warmed. "Riker, Marissa's out in the barn. Would you update her and ask her to join us?"

Like a shot, Riker and Ammo hurried down the steps, eager to escape the uncomfortable situation.

Walsh stood, ushering Dani into the house. "Riker means no disrespect or harm. He speaks what's on his mind."

"I appreciate candidness, but if your team has Jayne charged and convicted, I'm not sure they're the best to handle her case."

Walsh clamped his jaw tight to keep from retaliating. He knew she didn't mean that. "What did you overhear?"

"Enough. Someone's willing to pay for my death?"

"Yes."

Marissa, Riker, and Ammo returned to the house, interrupting the conversation.

Dani moved toward the porch rail, gazing out with her back to him. "Are we safe here?"

"It's best if you and Walsh go elsewhere," Riker replied. "I'll provide protection detail for Marissa."

"Negative." Marissa shook her head. "I'm not going anywhere."

"Did the assassination order mention Tessa?" Dani asked.

"No. Based on our intel, you're the mark," Riker explained.

Dani exhaled relief. She could bear the danger if Tessa wasn't the target. Walsh paced the kitchen.

"Eliana's working on the source of the hit," Riker said. "Honestly, it's not looking good. The person used the dark web, bouncing their IP address across Russia."

"Great," Dani groaned.

"We still have no leads on Aiden DeLuca. The dude vanished."

"Nobody disappears. Find him," Walsh said, realizing he sounded like a movie villain. "We'll head to the Rock."

"Roger that."

Walsh pulled his sister into a hug. "If there's any sign of danger, please don't be stubborn. Get out of here."

"I'll be fine," Marissa contested. "Finish this case. I can take care of myself."

"Humor me." He embraced her. "Do you need anything before we leave?"

"Nope. We're good."

Dani hugged Marissa goodbye, and they loaded Knox into the SUV.

Once they'd driven several miles from the ranch,

Dani said, "I won't run from an invisible assassin. Tessa's the priority. Are you certain she's safe?"

"We're praying so."

"I hope it's enough." *Lord, I need You.*

They'd driven several miles from the ranch when Walsh spotted a car billowing smoke on the shoulder of the road. The raised hood concealed the person before it.

"We should offer to assist."

"Armed." This could be a trap. Walsh holstered his gun, and Dani mimicked him.

He parked behind the sedan, activating the hazard lights, though the road was void of travelers. They exited the vehicle.

"Knox, stay," Dani said.

They cautiously approached. "Need help?" Walsh hollered.

A man stepped to the side, revealing himself and brandishing a pistol.

He aimed and shot at them.

Walsh and Dani dove for cover. They returned fire before bolting for the SUV. A second sedan screeched to a halt, blocking the SUV's driver's door. Two more assailants tumbled out of the vehicle.

Someone had set them up for an ambush!

# THIRTEEN

Knox clawed at the window, whining and barking.

Walsh and Dani returned shots again, shifting between the vehicles, trapping them.

Dani fired at the assailant beside the car in front of them. He yelled obscenities, confirming her bullet had made contact.

"I got him!" she hollered. "He's getting away!"

The sedan in front of Walsh's SUV sped from the scene in the opposite direction, tires squealing.

Walsh fired, shattering the driver's-door window of the vehicle behind them. Dani hit the grill, emitting steam.

"Go!" the driver of the second sedan yelled.

Both men dove into their car and reversed at high speed before swinging into a J-turn, racing from the scene. A wake of dust plumed in their path.

Walsh and Dani stood watching for a couple of seconds.

"Those guys orchestrated that ambush!"

"Was the hit a way to get us away from the ranch?" Dani asked.

"I'd say that's probable." He ushered Dani and Knox back into the SUV. "If they couldn't find where we were staying, they waited us out."

"Still, how did they know we'd be out here?"

Walsh didn't reply.

Knox leaned toward her, whining. "It's okay." Dani tried calming the frenzied animal, stroking his fur.

"Please call this into local PD while I get the team on the line."

Dani nodded, dialing 9-1-1. When she finished, Walsh was already in discussion with the task force on speakerphone.

"That's seriously disconcerting," Elijah replied.

"We're stuck here until LEOs arrive to take our report," Walsh advised.

"I'll stay here with Marissa, and we'll amp up the watch here at the ranch," Riker said.

"I'm also remote-monitoring the ranch cameras," Eliana noted.

"You have surveillance equipment on your property?" Dani asked aloud, regretting the interruption.

"Yes, after Marissa's attack, we added several, along with other safety features," Walsh replied.

"I've confirmed Meadowlark Lane's location and address are untraceable to you or Marissa's names," Eliana reported.

Dani would love to know how the computer tech had managed that move.

"Good job. My guess is our ambush was part of the paid hit on Dani," Walsh said. "Please continue digging."

"Roger that," Eliana replied. "Dani?"

"Yes?" Dani leaned closer.

"I have an update for you too. Were you aware that Jayne named you as Tessa's guardian in her living will?"

Dani gaped. "What?" She closed her eyes, absorbing the weight of the information. With Jayne's prognosis growing worse, she had to face the possibility that her friend might not live. "I... I'm not sure what to say." Her phone chimed with a text, and the team's voices faded into the background as she read the words.

Aiden DeLuca dies if you don't give me back the guns Jayne stole from me.

The screen displayed No Caller ID, and the number comprised only five digits. She snapped a screenshot and sent it to Eliana.

"Eliana, are you seeing this?" Dani asked.

A gasp came over the line. "Yes."

"Care to fill us in?" Walsh leaned closer.

Dani passed him the cell, and the color drained from his face.

"Why is there no real phone number?" she asked.

"The person is using a messaging program to conceal it," Eliana replied.

The team rapid-fired questions.

"Is it a trap?" Walsh asked.

"Did Aiden take the guns and run?" Tiandra asked.

"That makes sense," Chance replied.

"It stands to reason the text is from Enrique Prachank," Skyler said.

What did that mean for Jayne? Dani withheld the question.

"I think Sky is right," Elijah said. "He's got the

most to lose here, and we've already connected him to some of the missing evidence."

"The message says Jayne stole the weapons," Graham pointed out. "Is he implicating her or throwing her under the bus after she helped him?"

"We don't know that she was working with Prachank," Dani snapped, instantly regretting her emotional response. Riker's words bounced to the forefront of her mind, and she couldn't deny he was correct. She had lost focus for the sake of loyalty.

A second message pinged.

Come alone or he dies.

"Aiden is the only link we have," Dani said.

"But we don't have the guns," Elijah interjected. "You can't show up there empty-handed."

"We'll figure it out. We need Prachank," Dani replied.

"We could meet you and establish our own ambush," Riker said.

"Negative," Walsh said. "Riker, stay with Marissa until I release you. If this is a trap, we're not taking any chances."

"I concur," Dani said, reading her response aloud as she typed it.

Fine. Jayne told me everything. If you harm Aiden, no deal.

"Well done," Walsh said.

Drive to Iowa. Will send directions along the way. Share your location via your phone app.

"He's having us follow breadcrumbs," Dani said.

"He's ensuring we can't get there ahead of him." Walsh slammed his hand on the dashboard.

Knox poked his head through the divider.

"Sorry, buddy." Walsh stroked the dog's fur.

"We have Knox for help, too," Dani replied. "I'm going."

"*We're* going," Walsh said emphatically.

"But how will you show up without being seen?" Elijah asked.

"I'll figure it out on the way," Walsh quipped.

"Keep your phones on so we have GPS tracking," Eliana said.

"Roger that. We'll be in touch," Dani said.

Walsh straightened. "First, we pray."

The group's voices rose in prayer for safety, protection, wisdom and resolution. At the collective amen, Dani felt empowered. They disconnected just as local law enforcement arrived to take their report of the shooting.

"I'll handle this and get us on the road," Walsh said, exiting the vehicle.

Dani twisted around, facing Knox. "Did Jayne really do this?" she wondered aloud. "And how am I supposed to be a mother for Tessa if Jayne doesn't survive?"

Knox offered his tender, compassionate gaze.

What choice did she have? Jayne had listed Dani

as Tessa's guardian, transferring the complete responsibility of her only child to Dani. Had she updated her will before their most recent conversation? The promise Dani had made to her friend to care for Tessa suddenly fell into place. Jayne's trust in Dani spoke of the love and friendship between the women. Tessa was the most precious part of Jayne's heart. If she died, Dani owed it to her to ensure Tessa's happiness and health.

Yet, the insecurity creeped into her mind again, reminding Dani of her failures in marriage with Mark. She wasn't mother material.

Instead, she'd make the ultimate sacrifice and find the best home in the world for Tessa, with proper parents who'd devote their lives to caring for her. That was the only correct option.

Her job was to ensure justice for Jayne, regardless of the outcome. She refused to believe Jayne had willingly gotten involved with a known fugitive criminal for the sake of weapons trafficking. Jayne was innocent in this, or at the very least, her involvement was based on coercion or threats. She wouldn't endanger Tessa.

Still, Jayne had thought ahead, naming Dani in her living will. Had Jayne feared for her life? Did twentysomething women make wills? She'd never considered that when she was Jayne's age. *Lord, please heal her.*

Years of working in law enforcement had worn on her. She was tired of dealing with the dregs of society. Maybe being a full-time mother to Tessa was possible. She could take an early retirement.

She glanced up, catching her reflection in the visor mirror. Hope, dread, and fears mingled in her mind. Husbands left, but just as she'd stayed faithfully by her mother's side, Tessa might do the same. Her adopted daughter wouldn't abandon her.

Resolved, Dani closed her eyes and prayed for the courage to walk through her biggest fear. If she faced that hurdle, she'd take care of the innocent baby who had stolen her heart.

Dread consumed Walsh. For the hundredth time since Dani received the kidnapper's text, he debated turning around. "We should reevaluate. Let's slow down and develop a solid plan rather than cower to this maniac's demands."

"What other options are there?" Dani argued. "If we don't comply, Aiden DeLuca dies. Worse, Tessa, Jayne, and I ultimately remain in danger. We've got one shot at taking this guy down. It's the first time he's crawled out from under his rock. Our phones have GPS capabilities and Knox has an AirTag on his collar. Your team's tracking our location."

At the mention of his name, the Dobie mix popped his head between the divider doors.

Walsh couldn't dispute Dani's reasoning. "This is probably a trick. When Prachank discovers we don't have what he wants, things will get ugly."

"We'll convince him we took precautions as our insurance. We haven't got the weapons, but we'll lead him to them. Then HFTF does the takedown." Dani's phone chimed again. "Turn on Highway 20 east-bound."

Walsh complied with the instructions randomly forcing them on and off county roads and highways. "He's playing games."

"He's using the share location app to trace us. The ridiculous zigzagging ensures we're not being followed and that we don't call ahead for backup."

Again, Dani's logical reasoning made sense.

"Should I worry that you think like a criminal?" Walsh teased.

"Maybe." She joked and glanced down at a new text message. "Turn into Boone and drive to Ledges State Park," she instructed Walsh.

"He's taking us to an open space?"

"Ledges has trails and bluffs."

"High ground to oversee his prey. Great." He didn't hide his sarcasm.

She read the next text aloud. "'Park at the Ledges' lower lot until I give you further instructions.'"

Walsh pulled into the empty parking area. Not surprising, considering it was a weekday morning, but disconcerting, nonetheless.

Dani texted, advising they'd arrived.

"I don't like this."

"You've made that clear," she quipped. Her phone chimed again.

Hike Lost Lake Trail and wait under the shelter.

They exited the SUV and Walsh leashed Knox while Dani snagged a portable bowl and bottled water from the team's supply box. She tucked the items into her purse and they trekked the path. Humidity hung thick and their boots crunched on the dirt. At the divide in the trail, they paused. Stone steps led upward while the other direction offered a descent around the lake.

"Any preference?" Dani asked.

"Higher ground always," Walsh said.

Ascending the narrow steps surrounded by thick foliage, neither spoke, listening for danger. Birds trilled happily from the copse of trees.

Signs depicting Lost Lake Trail guided them, taking them on a shift in direction as they made the descent around a small body of water.

"Resembles a big pond." Dani swatted at a swarm of assaulting mosquitos.

Soft green moss blanketed the lake and low-hanging tree limbs hovered over the calm water. "That's too generous. It's swamplike," Walsh said.

A metal shelter with a table stood on the opposite side.

"Let's do a little recon before we move under that," Walsh suggested. "Have Knox search for explosives."

"Good idea."

They parted, scooting into the foliage. Knox cleared the area without issue, concluding their mission, and they entered the shelter.

"The silence is unnerving." Dani tugged Knox closer.

A dragonfly buzzed past Walsh's face. Frogs croaked in the distance, filling the atmosphere with their calls.

Dani filled the collapsible travel bowl from her purse with water. "I'm grateful your team stores canine supplies in all the vehicles."

Walsh smiled.

A message dinged on Dani's phone. She passed the device to Walsh.

Where are the guns?

He was watching them. Not that Walsh expected anything less.

Dani replied.

Will take you to them.

Again, the cell pinged with a text and her eyes widened as she read it. She turned it to Walsh. "We need to get out of here."

The message—You lied!—included a picture of Walsh and Dani standing beside the lake.

The angle implied Prachank stood on the same level as they did.

"Get to higher ground," Walsh said.

Gunshots exploded, rupturing tree bark next to them.

Walsh pulled Knox closer, and the trio dashed behind a large boulder.

They bolted up the narrow passage bordering the

lake to the stone steps. Bullets flew around them from what seemed like random directions.

Dani cried out.

Walsh turned to see her splayed out on the path.

"Are you hit?"

"I tripped, I'm fine! Go!"

He helped Dani to her feet, and they resumed their escape.

"Wait!" Dani withdrew her phone and deactivated the location sharing app. "Okay."

Walsh spotted a lesser traveled trail, descending to the Des Moines River. Stone walls and crevices offered hiding places.

They hiked down the steep embankment to a large opening in the rock. Ducking inside, they repositioned to peek out.

"Is he gone?" Dani kept Knox beside her.

The stillness lingered around them.

"I think so." Walsh withdrew his phone and frowned. "Of course, I have no reception here."

"How long do we wait?"

"If he's watching for us to materialize, let him believe he lost us."

Birds resumed their nature calls and, after twenty minutes, they emerged from their hiding place.

"Use the river to trace back to the parking area," Walsh suggested. "If he's waiting on the path, he'll trap us."

"Agreed."

They trekked the gravelly embankment, searching for purchase on the sandy shore. Frothy scum plagued the water, and the cliffs concealed them if the assailant stalked from overhead.

They reached an opening between the bank and river. Climbing through the thick foliage to the path, they paused. Knox sniffed a leafy bush.

Walsh leaned closer, detecting what had captured the dog's attention. "It's a casing!"

He used a stick to collect and pocket the evidence.

They cautiously trekked to the main road and finally reached the parking lot. Someone had shattered the windows and broken into the SUV.

"Thanks for not slashing these tires," Walsh mumbled sarcastically.

"I'd call this in, but I have no cell phone reception."

"Take pictures to document the scene."

They worked together, capturing images on their phones.

Walsh started the engine, voicing aloud a prayer of thanks that the attacker hadn't messed with the vehicle's mechanics. He cleaned a place for Knox while Dani did the same, brushing off the glass from the seats.

"Hey, Walsh?"

"Yeah?"

Knox sniffed at the section between the door and the floorboard. Walsh used his cell's flashlight app, illuminating a small piece of yellowed paper. Snapping a picture first, he donned a latex glove from the equipment stash and withdrew the sheet. "It's ten digits." He held it up for her to see.

"I recognize the 202-area code. It's a Washington,

DC, number. Good job, Knox," Dani cooed. "Let's get out of here and call it."

They loaded into the SUV and drove out of the park.

Once Walsh's cell showed service, he said, "Please dial the team on speakerphone."

"We lost track of you!" Eliana exclaimed when she answered.

"We had no reception in the area." Walsh offered a quick explanation of events.

"That's why he chose the location," Elijah observed. "He planned to trap you and steal the weapons."

"He made them hike, allowing time to break into the SUV," Riker replied.

"If he intended to kill us, he had the opportunity," Dani said.

"Shooting is Prachank's MO," Walsh said. "Breaking into the SUV is not."

"Prachank is more in-your-face," Tiandra agreed. "He's likely to attack you on the road, as those creeps did earlier."

"Nothing registers with this case," Dani grunted.

"We're returning with the casing," Walsh replied. "Skyler, you'll need to run it ASAP."

"Roger that," she responded.

Walsh continued, "Riker, try to convince Marissa to go with you to the Rock. If she refuses—"

"Actually, sir," Riker interrupted, "Marissa already booted me off the ranch. I'm at the Rock."

"I wish that surprised me," Walsh groused.

Dani smirked.

"We're monitoring the ranch's video feed," Eliana assured.

"Thank you," Walsh said.

"Before we end this call, Dani's texting a picture of a piece of paper Prachank or whoever broke into the SUV left. Whether on purpose or accidentally, we're not sure."

"You think it was intentional? As in the reason for the break-in?" Riker asked.

"Possibly." Dani swiped at the screen and forwarded the text. "Eliana, can you reverse trace the number?"

"Absolutely," she answered.

"That's the ATF headquarters office!" Skyler blurted.

Dani and Walsh exchanged a confused look.

"You're certain?" Walsh asked.

"Yes!" Skyler said.

"Why would Prachank leave that?" Graham asked.

"Dig into it," Walsh ordered.

"We're on it!" Chance assured him.

They disconnected, and Walsh faced Dani. "Where do we go from here?"

"This will tell us everything." She used a latex glove, lifting the casing to study it. "It's different. I've not seen this before."

"The whole investigation feels that way."

They drove in silence for several miles.

"We're covered."

"For now," Dani said. "But at some point, I have to

face the fact that Jayne might not make it out of this alive or free from prison."

Surprised by her admission, Walsh listened, not daring to speak.

"Am I delusional to be Tessa's guardian?" The whisper resembled a rhetorical question.

Walsh was unsure whether to answer. At her probing look, he took the cue. "You're capable of doing anything you set your mind to."

Their gazes held for several seconds. "Thank you," she said, giving his arm a gentle squeeze.

Walsh didn't move, though her touch sent electric shocks through him. The image of the two of them caring for Tessa as a family flashed before him.

And it scared him speechless.

# FOURTEEN

Dani's knee ached from the fall she'd taken at Lost Lake the day before, but she wouldn't complain. Eager to check on Tessa, she hurried into the HFTF building, Knox at her side.

"Where's the fire?" Walsh teased.

"Sorry." She held the door open for him.

Refreshed from a full night of exhausted sleep at the condo, she couldn't wait to hold Tessa.

They stopped to see the baby first, greeted with smiles from Troopers Ulrich and Nguyen.

"Hello sweet girl!" Dani pulled Tessa close.

"She's so much fun," Trooper Nguyen said.

"Thank you both. I'd like to take her upstairs for a little while," Dani said.

"We'll give you both a short break." Walsh smiled.

"Roger that," Ulrich replied with a yawn. "She was up early this morning."

Walsh and Dani hurried to the Rock. The team hadn't arrived yet. Dani dropped into the closest chair, surprised when Walsh sat beside her and reached for Tessa. "May I?"

Dani hesitantly passed the infant to him.

Tessa seemed tiny in his massive arms. He gently patted her back, laughing as she poked at his short hair.

"This is the first I've seen you interact with Tessa," Dani said.

He made funny sounds, eliciting the child's laughter. "Couldn't tell you she's my kryptonite."

Dani blinked. "You like kids?" She'd assumed the opposite.

"Of course. Once dreamed of having a huge family." He glanced at her over Tessa's head. "Losing that hope left me hesitant to connect with any child. But after talking with my bossy sister," he paused with a grin, "I realized keeping a distance is ridiculous."

"I had you all wrong."

"Hopefully, that's a good thing," he said.

Dani smiled. "It is." Even though the glimpse into his heart added to her growing attraction, his comment reactivated her self-protection shield. Walsh had wanted a family, something they wouldn't have in common. Mark had claimed he didn't want children. Then he'd divorced Dani, married another woman, and fathered several kids. Just like her father had done to her mother. She shoved away the unpleasant thoughts.

"Those days are gone with retirement knocking," Walsh interrupted.

"What's the mandatory age for the marshals?"

"Fifty-seven. I've got four years left." He snorted. "They'll take my badge and my identity. In my mind, I'm still twenty-five. Although my body claims a much older version of me." He laughed and made another silly face at Tessa.

"I'm right behind you with no idea what to do when I'm not employed anymore."

"Me either. Sometimes that scares me more than

the danger I've faced." Walsh's heartfelt confession touched Dani.

The team arrived, interrupting their discussion. Once they'd assembled around the table, Walsh called the meeting to order. "We need a lead to move forward. The attacks don't coincide with one kidnapper."

Chance added, "If Prachank has Aiden, who bombed the cave in Decorah?"

"Someone had access to the missing cache of munitions, and he's used some of them on us," Walsh noted. "Additionally, he's kept up with our locations, and that concerns me." He faced Eliana.

She took the cue, jumping into the discussion. "Dani's department-issued cell was most likely how the bomber traced you."

"No way. It's gotta be Walsh's?" Dani said, cringing inwardly at her defensiveness.

"His is a possibility," Eliana conceded. "However, we encrypt our devices. For safety reasons, it's best we move you both to burner phones."

"I don't know..." Dani argued. Having her phone taken away was like having an appendage removed. She needed it to do her job at GIPD, and it was also her link to Jayne. She hated being reliant on a device, but she didn't want to surrender it.

"Not a problem," Walsh said, sliding his cell across the table to Eliana.

Dani considered the request. "Can't we deactivate the GPS tracking or something?"

"Negative," Eliana said. "The alternative is to keep it powered off unless you're actively using it. However, as soon as you turn it on, the signal will ping the closest cell tower. If that's how the bomber is tracing you, you've provided him a map to your location."

Dani withdrew her phone and glanced down. "What about transferring calls from my line to the new burner?"

"I can do that." Eliana frowned. "It's still a risk."

"I'd prefer that for now. The hospital has this number and if Jayne's condition changes, I don't want there to be a delay in getting ahold of me. I also have responsibilities at Grand Island and can't be unavailable should someone need to reach me."

"Understandable." Eliana nodded. "I'll get to work on that right away."

"I have updates from my ATF contact," Skyler said. The team gave her their full attention. "They've analyzed the material collected from the explosion in Decorah, and the casing you provided yesterday from Ledges State Park. They confirmed the munitions used at the ice cave were military grade."

"The same ones from the missing cache?" Dani asked.

"Yes," Skyler said. "And get this, the casing from Ledges is from a scoped rifle. Here's the kicker. The gun is a special design, unique to one gunsmith in Winterset, Iowa."

"Outstanding work!" Walsh commended. "Sounds like we're making a trip to Winterset?"

"Actually, I've got the gunsmith's contact information if you'd rather call him," Eliana said.

"Yes, please." Walsh chuckled.

Skyler smirked. "You won't believe this. Floyd Arming."

Dani grinned. "Is that a real name?"

"Yep. Mr. Arming makes guns," Skyler replied.

Eliana quickly patched the number through the conference call system. The line rang three times before a man answered.

"Good morning. May I speak with Floyd Arming?" Walsh asked.

"You already are," Floyd replied.

"Sir, this is deputy US marshal, Commander Beckham Walsh, with the Heartland Fugitive Task Force. I'm calling regarding a scoped rifle you constructed. I'd like to send you a picture, if that's okay?"

"Absolutely. This is my cell phone."

Walsh gave Eliana a jerk of his chin, and within seconds, her message pinged.

"Got it," Floyd said. "Yep, that was a special order."

Walsh's gaze traveled around the room, meeting the team's surprised expressions. "How many did you make?"

"Just that one."

"Do you remember the buyer?" Walsh asked.

"Gimme a second to pull up my records," Floyd said. "I never forget a face, but names don't stick as well in my mind."

While they waited, Walsh whispered to Eliana, "Have Prachank's picture ready."

She nodded.

Floyd returned. "Yep, John Smith."

Walsh groaned. "I don't suppose you asked for his identification."

"Marshal, I always ask for ID. I run a reputable business."

Dani flicked a glance at Walsh and gave a slight shake of her head.

"My apologies," Walsh blurted. "With such a common name, I wonder if you'd recognize him if we sent a photo?"

"Never forget a face," Floyd replied.

Walsh nodded at Eliana, and she texted the picture.

"Hmm, nope. That's not the guy," Floyd said.

Dani gaped. If not Prachank, then…

"May I show you another possibility?" Walsh asked then mouthed *Aiden* to Eliana. A second ping.

"Yep, that's him," Floyd confirmed.

Dani met Walsh's gaze. A small measure of satisfaction welling inside her.

"Sir, you've been very helpful," Walsh said. "Thank you."

"Happy to help. You want the contact information he gave me?" Floyd asked.

"That would be great." Walsh jotted down the data Floyd provided. He thanked the gunsmith again, and they disconnected. "Looks like Aiden DeLuca has an address in Council Bluffs, Iowa."

"That answers part of the mystery," Graham said.

Dani noticed how he didn't mention Jayne, but she bit her lip from commenting. Instead, she said, "Stands to reason that Aiden DeLuca played everyone. Weapons contractor turned arms dealer under the assumed name John Smith?"

"He had the connections and understood the law well enough to stay below the radar," Riker said.

"Hold on. The gun Aiden ordered and purchased doesn't prove who shot it. His kidnapper might've stolen it. Aiden's still missing." Walsh tapped the paper with Aiden's secondary address. "Unless we find him there." He rose and walked to the evidence board. "Any other leads? Other than the thief using his stash to try and kill me and Dani?"

The group shook their heads.

"Talk to Aiden's associates," Walsh suggested.

"We spoke with Omaha PD," Tiandra reported. "Everyone's complimentary of him."

"But they also said they've lost touch with him over the years. He wasn't a golfer, had no hobbies, and didn't have many friends," Graham added.

"On the other hand, if Aiden's a victim caught up in this mess, he's in danger," Walsh inserted. "When we didn't produce the weapons to his kidnapper, he might've grown desperate."

"You mean we might've got Aiden Deluca killed," Dani concluded.

"Dani and I will drive to Aiden's address in Council Bluffs," Walsh said. "If he's there, that'll tell us a lot."

"Yes." She offered an affirming nod. "Perfect. He won't expect us."

"Another thing," Skyler said. "The number you found is the ATF main line."

"If Aiden was the shooter at Ledges State Park, why would he have the ATF's contact info on him?" Graham inquired.

"I think he's busy making connections," Elijah added.

"Keep digging, people. We'll be in touch." Walsh got to his feet and Dani joined him, leashing Knox. They dropped off Tessa with the troopers before heading out of the building.

Once they were on the road, Walsh said, "Talk it out."

"What?"

"Your tumbling thoughts."

She sighed. "Aiden influenced and took advantage of Jayne. It's clear he's a liar and a manipulator."

"That's possible."

They bounced ideas around until they arrived at the address: a mobile home park. Walsh parked the SUV several homes from John Smith's—aka Aiden DeLuca's—unit. They exited the vehicle, and with Knox leashed, approached.

"Is Knox trained in apprehension?" Walsh asked.

Dani cringed. "We tried multiple disciplines as part of his repertoire. As you've witnessed, Knox is more about the comfort than the attack."

Walsh chuckled. "Aiden doesn't know that." He winked.

"Roger that. We'll take the back door."

They flanked the single-wide trailer, Dani and

Knox moved to the rear entrance. Walsh approached the front door and knocked.

Aiden answered, wearing shorts and a button-up shirt, surprise written on his face. He'd aged since Walsh had last seen him. More silver streaked the man's dark wavy hair, but Walsh had no doubt it was Aiden.

"Been a long time!" Walsh said.

The man blinked.

"Aiden DeLuca, right? From Omaha PD?" Walsh kept his tone light.

Aiden cleared his throat. "Yes." He glanced around, taking a small step backward, posture stiffening slightly.

"Not sure if you remember me. We only met twice."

Aiden paused for several seconds, then placed a hand over his mouth as though in thought before saying, "You're familiar, but I don't recall your name."

Walsh could tell Aiden was lying based on his telltale body language.

"Beckham Walsh." Walsh aimed for a casual lean on the metal porch railing. "Mind if I talk with you? I'm hoping you can help me with a case I'm working."

Another long pause. "Uh, sure. Come on in." Aiden stepped aside.

"Chief, we're clear," Walsh called out.

Dani and Knox rounded the house and walked to the steps, joining Walsh and Aiden. The man visibly swallowed again, offering a wary glance at Knox.

They entered the dated dwelling, decorated with lawn chairs leaning against the wall and a box television. Aiden gestured to the only proper furniture, a run-down recliner.

"We're fine here," Dani said, taking her position beside the door. Walsh moved toward the kitchen area, blocking the only other exit.

Aiden nodded. "So, what do you need my help with?"

"Heard you're doing weapons destruction for several agencies now…" Walsh began.

That seemed to calm Aiden, and he dropped onto the recliner. "Yeah. Would you like a bid for your department?"

"Actually…" Walsh stood feet shoulder-width apart, hands on his hips, drawing attention to his duty weapon. "Chief Fontaine and I are working on a case of missing munitions from the Grand Island PD."

Aiden remained silent, probably waiting on what they already had on him.

"You knew the evidence technician, Jayne Bardot?" Dani asked.

"Yes, I did." Aiden looked down. "We were involved."

"I'm curious why you're here under an assumed name," Walsh asked.

Aiden exhaled a breath, an indicator he was ready to confess. "Look, I know I messed up, but the thing is, they're trying to kill me."

"Who is?" Dani clarified.

"Jayne and Prachank."

Dani's posture stiffened, revealing her rising defenses. "Jayne is working with Prachank?"

"As in Enrique Prachank?" Walsh added.

Aiden nodded emphatically. "Yes. They cooked up this plan to steal the weapons and resell them on the black market. Jayne pretended to care for me, then threatened my life if I didn't give them the munitions in my possession for destruction."

"How did she threaten you?" Disbelief etched Dani's expression and was clearly discernible in her tone.

"With a gun and intimidation," Aiden said. "As I explained, we were in a relationship. Initially, I was oblivious that Jayne was using me to get to the firearms. If it hadn't been for Tessa, I would've turned her in to the authorities, but I didn't want to see little Tessa become an orphan because of her mother's bad choices."

Dani glared at Aiden but said nothing more.

"Is she okay?" Aiden met Walsh's gaze. His eyebrows creased in concern.

"Jayne?" Walsh responded.

"Tessa. That poor sweet baby. I adore her."

If Jayne and DeLuca were in a relationship, wouldn't she have told Dani? Though Walsh wanted to ask, he refrained. A twinge of doubt lingered. If Aiden was telling the truth, it explained Jayne's deception.

"I'd love to see Tessa. I've been worried sick since learning about Jayne's injuries," Aiden continued.

That got Walsh's attention. "Where did you hear that?"

Aiden frowned. "You've been in law enforcement long enough. Officers talk. It's an active grapevine. I have a solid reputation in the community, even after my forced retirement." A bitterness hung in Aiden's words.

Walsh couldn't dispute the comment. Cops talked, and it wasn't as if the shooting was a secret. Aiden seemed sincere. Walsh noticed the way Dani had cringed at Aiden's asking about Tessa.

"So, you're hiding out here because you fear for your life?" Walsh clarified.

"I should've gone to the police, but after Jayne was shot, I got scared. Prachank's coming for me. Once word gets out about the missing munitions I was supposed to destroy, that will cost me my job. I need your help!" Aiden straightened in the recliner. "And I'll do whatever you want for the investigation. Just please get those weapons back before I lose everything. Criminals stole my career from me with this stupid permanent disability. I've had to rebuild my life once. I cannot face doing that again." Aiden's eyes shimmered.

"Why did you use an assumed name to purchase a gun from Floyd Arming?" Walsh asked, determined to take Aiden off guard.

The man's head shot up so fast, Walsh wondered if he'd get whiplash. "You know about the rifle?" Something in his demeanor spoke of deceit.

They had him cornered. What would he confess?

"Yes." Dani stepped closer. "Now's a good time to tell us the truth."

"I didn't want it traced back to me."

"You understand using fake identification to purchase a firearm is punishable under the law?" Dani asked.

"It was a gift for Jayne."

Dani used one hand to rub her eyebrow. The guy couldn't possibly be serious. "Why would you buy Jayne a gun under an assumed name?"

"Because I love her, and she asked me to. She didn't want it traced to either of us. I used some of my contacts, called in favors…" He shrugged, letting his voice trail off.

Walsh flicked a glance at her. It was plausible but, based on her frown and the contempt covering her expression, Dani wasn't buying it.

"Why wouldn't Jayne tell anyone about your relationship?" Dani asked.

Aiden appeared hurt. "Maybe she was ashamed of me? Especially since I'm not a cop anymore. Thanks to a forced early *retirement*—" he spat the word as though it burned his tongue "—for medical issues I sustained working a case." He looked down, intertwining his hands. "Can't blame her."

Pity filled Walsh for the guy. More than one officer had talked to him about the hardship of losing their identity after handing over the badge. Wasn't that his own fear?

"Seriously, though, is Tessa okay?" Aiden's gaze bounced between them.

"Yes, she's in protective custody," Walsh replied.

Aiden nodded. "That's good."

"I'll have to charge you with providing false statements to acquire a firearm, at a minimum," Walsh advised. "That gun was also used in the commission of a crime, namely, to shoot at police officers."

Aiden gaped. "No! Was anyone hurt?"

"That's irrelevant," Dani snapped.

"I'm guilty of buying the weapon for Jayne, but I gave it to her. I did it under duress and coercion."

"You'll have to work that out with your defense attorney," Walsh informed him.

Aiden hung his head. "I understand. Are you arresting me?"

Walsh and Dani exchanged looks. "Yes."

Unable to take Aiden in his patrol unit, Walsh lifted his phone and called the local authorities. Once they'd assured him they were on the way, he addressed Aiden, "You'll be charged and detained at the Council Bluff PD."

# FIFTEEN

Walsh focused on the road and inhaled deeply while Dani ranted about Aiden. She needed time, space and freedom to vent, but like a bulldog with a fresh bone, she wasn't letting it go.

"He's lying!" Dani exclaimed in the SUV as they drove back to Omaha. "Aiden is a dirtbag criminal! He's got every reason in the world to pin all of this on Jayne. Especially since she's unable to defend herself against his allegations." She harrumphed and crossed her arms.

Walsh counted to three before saying, "We have no evidence to refute what he told us. His account has credence." He maintained external calmness. Inwardly, he stifled annoyance at Dani's infuriatingly stubborn belief about Jayne's innocence.

If anything, Walsh was more inclined to believe Aiden. He'd seen more than one person travel that slippery slope in the name of love. What would it take for Dani to see that her friend was involved in all of this?

They entered the Omaha city limits without further discussion. By the time he turned onto Harney Street, entering the Old Market neighborhood, Dani's posture had softened. He activated his turn signal and prepared to pull into the headquarters' underground parking garage.

"Let's update the task force and—" An explosion cut off Walsh.

As though someone pressed the slow-motion button, a dust cloud swirled from the upper floors of the HFTF building.

The resounding boom lingered.

Concrete debris landed on Walsh's vehicle, coinciding with the volatile thud.

The SUV rocked, and smoke emitted from the hot engine.

Walsh blinked, trying to focus against the mess and to process the unbelievable devastation before his eyes. He turned to face Dani.

She sat, mouth agape, staring at the building. "Tessa!"

Walsh wasted no time grabbing his phone and reporting the incident. "Send fire and rescue now!" he hollered, not waiting for the 9-1-1 dispatcher to respond, and tossed the cell into his shirt pocket.

He shifted into Park, and then processed the SUV wasn't going anywhere. Thrusting open his door, Walsh jumped out, leaving the impaled vehicle in the center of the road. Dani exited on her side and leashed Knox.

They rushed toward the building and entered the foyer.

Dust and smoke assailed them, making breathing difficult.

Fire alarms blared and the overhead sprinklers sprayed water to extinguish a blaze that didn't exist.

"There's a north and south stairwell," Walsh announced. The troopers were on the second floor, and the Rock was located on the fourth. They couldn't be in two places at once.

"Check on the team. I need to find Tessa! I'll take the north." Dani spun on her heel and sprinted for the door.

Walsh hurried up the south stairwell, taking three steps at a time. When he reached the fourth level, he shoved open the doors and entered the Rock. Smoke billowed, blurring his vision and laboring his breathing. He covered his mouth using the neck of his undershirt.

"Team!" Walsh hollered at the top of his lungs, unable to see his hand in front of his face.

"Here!" Eliana called. She limped toward him, supported by Riker with Ammo at their side.

When they reached Walsh, he saw the dark stain that marred her right cheek. Black dust stained her pale blue blouse. His heart lurched. "Are you okay?"

"Yes. I'm fine. Ammo alerted. We didn't—" Eliana's voice trailed off and tears filled her eyes.

"Get out of here," Walsh ordered Riker, then paused. "Where is everyone else?"

Eliana turned to look at the space. "I'm not sure. We were all working in the office. Tiandra and—" Just as she spoke their names, Tiandra, K-9s Bosco and Destiny, and Chance, hurried up to them.

"Are you injured?" Walsh's inquiry came out more as a bark than a question.

"No," Chance said. "The wall collapsed beside us."

"Skyler and the Kenyon twins left a while ago to deal with Aiden," Tiandra reported.

"Get out of here." Walsh repeated the order. "Use the south stairwell. I'm heading to the second floor to check on Dani and the troopers."

He rushed down the steps with his teammates trailing behind and bolted through the stairwell door. He sprinted along the hallway, checking all the rooms. "Dani!"

No response. Had they already evacuated the building?

Fallen drywall had crushed Tessa's playpen.

Walsh sprinted forward, crying out for the baby and terrified of what he'd find. He skidded to a halt in front of it and glanced down.

Empty except for debris.

Walsh sent up a prayer of gratitude and exhaled relief.

He continued through the hallway, searching the gradually worsening destruction. Crushed walls and concave sections of the floor consumed the area. He stepped carefully around the holes where the first level was visible below.

Fire devoured a section of the east side, filling the atmosphere with more smoke.

Grateful to find no one injured, and confused at where they'd gone, he completed clearing the floor and hurried down the stairwell to the foyer.

He bolted outside, colliding with an entering firefighter. "Sorry, man. We cleared the second and fourth levels," Walsh instructed.

He nodded behind his SCBA mask and several more responders joined him, moving into the building.

Walsh sprinted to find Dani and his team members. They'd assembled outside at a safe distance. All stared at the burning, destroyed structure. Relieved to see Dani was okay, but sickened that she wasn't holding Tessa, Walsh sped up his approach.

"Walsh!" Anguish hung in Dani's voice as she rushed to him, arms outstretched. "She's gone! Someone kidnapped Tessa!"

"Where are Nguyen and Ulrich?" Walsh asked, trying to process what Dani had just told him.

"I found them unconscious in the hallway!" She pointed to the building. "We have to get them out."

"There's no one left," Walsh replied, confused. How had he missed the men?

Against the protests of the firefighters, Dani, Tiandra, and Walsh hurried back inside and up to the second level.

Dani gestured to the empty space. "They were right here!"

"I cleared the floor and never saw them," Walsh attested.

"Walsh! We found them," Tiandra shouted.

Walsh and Dani ran to meet Tiandra in the stairwell door. They followed her outside, spotting the two troopers sitting on the sidewalk beside Walsh's SUV. Both held their heads in their hands.

"They came down the south stairwell and rounded

the building," Tiandra explained. "Ya'll must've missed each other in the chaos."

Nguyen covered his mouth. "What seemed like a smoke bomb exploded and then everything went black," he was relating to Riker between hacking coughs. "The bomber must've laced it with some kind of chemical agent to knock us out."

"Where is Tessa?" Walsh demanded.

Ulrich blinked. "We couldn't find her when we came to. We thought you had her!"

Walsh withdrew his cell phone and ordered an Amber Alert for Tessa. Dani sank to the sidewalk, her head in her hands, and melted into inconsolable sobs.

Walsh stared, unable to reassure her or to fix the problem. He struggled with the worst case of helplessness he'd ever known.

Tiandra rushed to Dani's side to offer support. Riker spoke to him, but Walsh's ears were ringing and his mind whirled. He couldn't comprehend anything the man was saying. He looked at the building, baffled that someone had kidnapped baby Tessa and nearly killed his team while destroying their headquarters.

Questions plagued Walsh. How had the bomber gotten inside? Security cameras and electronic doors requiring badge entry secured the building.

Rescue personnel covered the area, rushing in and out, and working to extinguish the flames.

Walsh shifted into command mode, putting aside his fears and worries for Tessa. He approached the fire chief on scene and provided an account of the events. Once he'd established the necessity for them to contact him immediately should anything change, he turned to Dani.

"Team, we'll relocate to the condo as our temporary headquarters." Walsh glanced at Dani, and she nodded. "Our entire focus is on finding Tessa."

The HFTF members assembled in the living room of the condo. They created a base of operations with the remnants of their evidence board and collected documents.

The firefighters had cleared the scene, confirming multiple ignition devices had destroyed the HFTF headquarters. The source was still under investigation. Though she was a newcomer to the group, Dani felt the pain at seeing their devastation. She couldn't imagine how it affected the incredible team that had worked so hard to establish their space.

Her heart refused to linger on those thoughts when Tessa remained missing. Even with the Amber Alert, the chances of them finding the infant declined with every passing minute.

Dani clutched a stuffed raccoon Eliana had bought for the baby and paced beside the dining room table. Thankfully, Eliana and Riker had salvaged Eliana's laptop before leaving the office. It hadn't been damaged, unlike the rest of the reports and documents destroyed in the explosion. Still, Dani was grateful no lives were lost.

Skyler and the Kenyon twins arrived, bringing

food and supplies, while the team ran through the latest updates, catching them up on the situation.

"Where do we start?" Dani paced a path in the space.

"Based on what you and Walsh learned about Aiden DeLuca, do we believe Prachank is responsible for our headquarters bombing?" Riker asked.

"Aiden was in custody," Walsh said.

"Negative," Skyler said. "He bonded out before we got there."

"How's that possible?" Walsh's voice thundered.

"Dunno, but Council Bluffs PD released him," Graham said.

Convinced Aiden was involved, Dani blurted, "He had a connection at the PD." She didn't say it, but the implication was that the brotherhood had protected him. She'd seen it happen before when she'd worked for the Cortez PD. Part of the reason Chief Varmose had gotten away with his crimes for so long. "He's responsible for this."

"How?" Walsh barked. "There's no way they'd just let Aiden go."

Dani met his eyes, challenging him. "I disagree, and we can't exclude the possibility."

"That's ridiculous," Walsh snapped. "Your focus on Aiden is unreasonable."

"Excuse me?" Dani lifted her chin in defiance. "He bought the gun, using a fake ID, and stole weapons that were supposed to be destroyed."

"And he implicated Jayne in all of that as well," Walsh reminded her. "The man couldn't have gotten out of custody, rushed to the Rock ahead of us, blown up the building, and kidnapped Tessa. He's no supervillain."

"The bomb provided the distraction so he could kidnap her!" Dani retorted.

Aware the group was witnessing the exchange, Dani inhaled.

"No argument there," Eliana said softly. "I'm pulling our camera footage to see if there are any leads."

Dani and Walsh held each other in a silent standoff. The team quieted and worked the case in hushed tones.

"I need air." Walsh exited the condo, shutting the door a little harder than necessary.

Dani stared after him, then sheepishly faced the group. Did they think she was ridiculous? Her gaze flicked to Riker. He'd already voiced his opinion. Did the others feel the same way?

"Excuse me." Dani hurried to the bathroom, needing privacy to deal with the flood of emotions threatening to overtake her.

She closed the door and slid down the wall, cradling her head in her hands. Desperation and fear assailed her from every side. "Lord, I can't fix this, and I don't know where to look or who to blame. Please protect Tessa and somehow help us find her." She didn't try to stop the flood of tears. Her throat hurt from stifling the sobs so the others wouldn't hear her.

A rapping interrupted Dani's breakdown and she got to her feet. "Be right out." She washed her face and opened the door.

Walsh stood on the other side. A part of Dani wanted to slam the door, while the other sought to launch herself into his arms, seeking comfort.

He handed her a glass of water. "I thought you might want this."

Dani took the proffered drink. "Thank you." Stalling for time, she sipped at it and stepped out of the bathroom.

Walsh tucked his hands into his pockets, looking more like a teenager than a grown man nearing retirement. "Dani, I—"

She lifted her hand. "We're stressed. Let's just find Tessa."

His expression softened. They returned to the main room, where the team continued working.

"All right, where are we?" Walsh asked.

"We'll have to divide and conquer," Skyler said, taking the lead.

"We've got facial recognition sightings of Prachank all up and down the I-80 corridor," Eliana said.

"Real or staged?" Graham asked.

"Not sure," Eliana said. "Still searching for Aiden DeLuca."

"Then we need to follow up on all of them," Skyler said.

"Graham and I can start tracking those down," Elijah said.

"We've also received another report of evidence unaccounted for from Fremont PD," Eliana reported.

"Tiandra and I will tackle that," Riker said.

Dani remained silent.

"Good. You've got a great handle on this," Walsh commended.

Dani's cell phone rang with an unfamiliar number. She quickly answered, placing the call on speakerphone. Silence hung thick.

"Hello?"

"You will bring me the missing guns, or you'll never see this brat again," a mechanical voice ordered.

Dani's heart froze in her chest. The room spun, and she teetered. Walsh reached out a hand to ground her. Each member shifted closer, the group intently focused on the kidnapper's demand.

"I did that earlier, and you tried to kill me," Dani replied, forcing calmness into her tone.

Walsh waved wildly, trying to get her attention, but Dani ignored him. She would handle this her way and rescue Tessa. Dani refused to avert her gaze from the phone in front of her, as though Tessa's life hung in the balance of her cell's reception.

"You're playing games with me!" the kidnapper snarled.

"No, I'm not," Dani assured him. "I want Tessa back. I'll do whatever you ask."

"You said that before."

"You're right. I'm sorry for not bringing the guns, but I will make sure that you get them this time."

She glanced up, meeting Walsh's wide eyes.

Dani shook her head, reminding him she was bluffing. What other choice did she have?

"Good, I'm glad we're in agreement," the kidnapper said. "And if you come with that stupid mutt or the marshal, I will kill the baby."

Dani cringed at the horrible threat. "Understood. There's no need for that." She hated the quivering in her voice. "I'll bring you the guns. Tell me where."

"Drive to the location I text you and pick up the phone I'll provide for you. You'll get further directions then. Don't try pulling anything funny, or you'll be sorry. I'm watching you." The line disconnected.

"Hello? Hello?" Dani cried.

"Not happening." Walsh pinned her with a stare.

"I don't need your permission," Dani replied.

"What are you doing?"

"I'm getting Tessa. I'll do whatever it takes to make that happen."

"She's right," Tiandra proclaimed. "He has the upper hand. We must play along."

"He said he's watching." Eliana added, "We have no way to identify where he is."

"Correct. But we'll leave as a group and disperse. He can't follow us all," Walsh said.

"We need to distract him and trick him into thinking Dani is one of us and vice versa," Graham said. "A switcheroo. Then we'll have backup in the vehicle with her."

"No." Dani argued, "If he suspects we're trying something fishy, he'll kill Tessa. We can't risk that."

"We're not even sure what munitions he's talking about," Riker said.

"So we'll have to wing it," Elijah replied.

"Right!" Skyler confirmed. "Where's the list of missing weapons?"

Eliana jumped into the discussion. "That's part of the problem. We're finding more are unaccounted for from agencies around the state. There are reports coming in from North Platte, Norfolk, even as far as Scottsbluff."

Dani blinked, processing the information. All at once, the team blurted questions.

"What?"

"How?"

"When did it start?"

Walsh held up a hand to silence them.

"It's like an epidemic," Graham said. "Where do we start?"

"We'll borrow cases and bags from NSP. Make him think we have the munitions." Walsh fixated his glance on Dani. "You do what you've suggested already," he said to Skyler, "disperse and tackle all of them. We need to know exactly what's missing. My guess is that he wants the military stuff most, so let's focus on that for now."

"There was no more found at the ice cave. Whoever stole them hid the rest somewhere else," Tiandra said.

"What about Dani going alone?" Skyler asked.

"That's not happening," Walsh replied.

Though Dani wanted to argue with him, she was relieved he'd accompany her. Instinct said the kidnapper wouldn't hesitate to kill her.

"Let's go," Walsh ordered. "Eliana, please stay here

and continue working on the missing evidence reports and camera footage from the Rock."

"Roger that."

"I'll ride with Riker. We'll drive to the underpass near Fremont, and I'll get in with Dani at that point," Walsh advised. "We have the burner phones."

"Negative. If he has an electronic finder, you'll be made. We won't be able to track you beyond Dani's cell once she's forced to trade it out for the kidnapper's device," Eliana said.

"You want me to go in dark?" Walsh asked.

"You'll have to," Eliana responded.

*Great.* They were going in without backup or a way to call for help. "No. I'll go alone," Dani said. "You'll just have to trust me."

"It's not on you," Walsh replied.

"No!" Dani fixed her jaw. "I'm getting Tessa back." She grabbed the keys for one of the SUVs and stormed out the door.

# SIXTEEN

"We're running out of daylight," Walsh said. "You got eyes on Dani?" Knox panted from the passenger seat of Trooper Ulrich's beater sedan.

"Yep, the location is coming through clearly," Eliana replied over speakerphone. "She's headed west-bound toward Central City."

It had taken a lot of coercing, but Dani had finally relented to slipping a GPS tracker into her boot for them to trace. Eliana's brilliant suggestion had proved beneficial since Dani had traded her vehicle and cell phone two towns and sixty miles ago, presumably based on the kidnapper's instructions.

Walsh and Knox maintained a healthy distance, following Eliana's verbal directions, grateful for the flat landscape that allowed him to see far into the horizon. Unsure if Dani was alone or had been forced to ride with the criminal, they relied on the transmitting GPS for her location.

"They're still moving eastbound," Eliana advised.

"I'll stay out of sight." No way was he leaving Dani without backup and vulnerable to the criminal's ridiculous demands.

Knox whined.

"I agree, pal." Walsh patted the dog. "Don't worry, we'll catch up to her. I hate not having visual on her."

"You're about a quarter mile behind her," Riker replied.

Keystrokes preceded Eliana's voice. "Go north another mile and turn south. That will allow you to approach from the opposite end of the road."

"Looks like she stopped at an abandoned farm set on the next pivot corner. You'll have to hike in the rest of the way." Eliana referenced the section of land not covered by irrigation pivots.

"There's a wooded area about a half mile on the north side of the fields. The cornstalks will cover you too."

"Excellent." Walsh fought the urge to speed to the location, not wanting to attract attention to himself. He pulled in between the thick foliage as the last rays of sunlight faded into darkness. "I'm signing off. We're in the woods."

He disconnected from the team call and withdrew binoculars from the console.

Knox sat upright, anxious. "Stay here." Walsh pushed open his door and surveyed the surroundings.

True to Eliana's assessment, in the distance, he spotted the caving roof of a dilapidated house. Dani had assured him that Knox understood commands for silent approach, and he prayed the dog cooperated with him.

He shut off his phone, leaving it behind. Eliana had warned if the kidnapper had any electronic detection devices, he'd trace Walsh.

He had to go in dark.

Opening the passenger door, he released Knox and snapped on his vest and leash. They trekked over the uneven ground and ducked into the maturing cornfields. The chest-tall stalks forced Walsh to approach in a crouched position.

Walsh and Knox zigzagged between the thick rows of crops. The field bordered the house's property with its wide dirt driveway.

He spotted an old car, most likely what Dani had driven based on the kidnapper's orders, parked near a barn. She was nowhere in sight. Fear had his heart triple beating against his rib cage. Where had she gone?

He paused behind the last complete row of corn and offered Knox the hand signal Dani provided for silence. Even the dog's panting had quieted.

No movement or lights anywhere on the property. At the far side stood a large barn. In the distance, he spotted a gardening shed with stacks of wood leaning against it.

Walsh inhaled deeply. With Knox close to him, he exited the safety of the foliage. They advanced in measured steps, keeping within the shadows of the two-story farmhouse. Its crumbling wraparound porch held a rotting bench and the front door stood ajar.

Had she gone inside? Why?

With a last glance over his shoulder, Walsh clung to Knox's leash and lunged into the open area, crossing to the house.

He neared the porch steps.

A whizzing and slight *pfft* rang out behind him.

Knox barked and Walsh turned just as something pierced his back. His fingers went numb, and he dropped the leash. "Find Dani!"

Knox woofed again and bolted through the door.

In a flash, Walsh's knees weakened.

He reached around to his right hip, withdrawing the brightly colored tranquilizer dart. The world spun.

He struggled to maintain consciousness against the thick lure dragging him down. His arms and legs went numb, unwilling to obey his mind's command to run for his life.

From the depths of the darkness, the pitiful, desperate wails of a baby reached him. Tessa!

Then Knox barking.

All of it too far away.

Walsh opened his mouth to speak, but nothing came out. He laid down, arm outstretched, and closed his eyes, surrendering to the chemical.

A piercing headache thrust Walsh awake. He struggled to drag himself from the intoxication still swirling in his system, unsure how long he'd been unconscious. His eyelids were tight, almost glued shut, and he had to work to open them. He squinted, allowing time for his vision to adjust.

Walsh replayed the last few moments, recalling that he'd fallen on the porch steps thanks to a tranquilizer dart.

Dani's empty car.

Knox barking and Tessa's cries.

Suddenly wide awake, Walsh sat up and winced, surveying his surroundings. Only a fragment of light cut through the inky room, revealing the wooden floor. He twisted to see the splintering workbench behind him. Both his wrists were bound tightly behind his back and flexi-cuffs strapped his ankles in front of him.

"Knox," he rasped against the dryness in his throat. Nothing.

In the distance, the familiar barks reached him. "Knox!" Would the dog hear him? Where was he?

His hip ached where the tranquilizer dart had hit him, leaving the lingering wooziness. "Knox!"

Walsh scooted forward, using both boots planted firmly on the floor. A tiny rectangular window on the opposite side explained the dim light cast across the wooden planks. He scanned for a door. Plastic bags of soil and other tools consumed the room. He surmised he was inside the gardening shed he'd seen earlier.

"Dani! Knox!" Fear and dread warred within Walsh.

The kidnapper had watched in a cat-and-mouse game the entire time. He'd waited for Walsh to emerge, then shot him with the tranquilizer dart. Why not shoot to kill? Because he wasn't the target. Dani was.

Was she alive? Hurt?

Walsh's stomach roiled. Why hadn't he been more careful? Knox had run off, but to where? Was the dog okay?

He'd failed again! Dani was at the mercy of a madman choreographing dangerous games. And when the kidnapper found out the bags and boxes in the car weren't guns, he'd kill her.

If he could do it all over, he'd find a hundred different ways to confess his feelings for Dani. He wouldn't have dodged her. What a coward he'd been! Playing warrior on the other side of the world, yet too afraid to face the woman he'd loved more than half of his life.

"Please God, grant me a second chance." Walsh tugged against his restraints, desperate to escape. He had to help Dani!

Unable to stand, he inched along the shed floor, searching for a way out. He tried to separate his feet, using body weight to break free. The bindings remained fixed around the base of his ankles, restricting him from even withdrawing his foot from inside the boot.

It occurred to Walsh that he'd not heard Knox barking any more. The silence encroached on him, bringing with it fears of the unknown.

Like his future that sat on that same plain. "Lord, I'm afraid." He'd never confess that. Not during his military deployments or any undercover operation he'd worked in the past.

*Lean not unto your own understanding.* The words flitted to mind unbidden, providing Walsh the direction he needed. "I've existed in a comfortable place, hiding behind my badge and title. Those things will be stripped away soon. Lord, that scares me. Who am I without them?"

Exhausted, Walsh closed his eyes.

Aiden DeLuca was proof that once Walsh transitioned into a civilian role, he'd eliminate his entire identity and all he'd known for the past three decades. Not that his badge helped him now.

He hadn't guarded Dani or rescued Tessa. His life would end, realizing his worst fears. He'd failed again.

Hopelessness consumed Walsh, and he leaned his head against the hard wooden wall.

Images of Dani played before his eyes. Marissa was right. He'd loved Dani for as long as he could remember.

His ambitions had provided amazing opportunities. The epiphany flashed as bright as a light before him. The accolades and career titles hadn't kept him going. It was the unquenchable need to help others. Hadn't God given Walsh that calling? Then only He could remove it, not some criminal.

No. He wouldn't give up.

Walsh stretched his ankles to the maximum distance, finally hearing the flexi-cuffs snap free. Exhilarated, he scooted against the shed wall. With his hands still bound behind his back, Walsh inched upward until he was standing.

Relieved, he searched for something to cut through the bindings, simultaneously examining the space for the door to escape.

A scream erupted outside, searing his heart. "Dani!"

Knox's familiar bark reached Dani as she climbed the steps of the old farmhouse. She turned, setting the bags with the fake weapons down on the floor.

"Knox?" The Dobie mix rushed to her side.

She dropped beside him, hugging his panting frame. "Where did you come from?" Dani spoke the words aloud for the kidnapper's benefit, fully aware Walsh had followed her.

This wasn't the plan, though.

If the kidnapper saw Knox, he'd assume she'd ignored his rules. Irritation swirled with fear. Had something happened to Walsh? Surely, he wouldn't have released Knox voluntarily.

Her throat constricted.

The criminal's directions had ordered her to ascend the steps to the second floor of the house and leave the bags in the bedroom on the left. In the dark, she scanned the area, wishing she'd grabbed a flashlight before switching vehicles. Another of the ridiculous demands, along with leaving her cell phone.

The cheap burner phone he'd provided was her only method of communication. She prayed the team was still monitoring the GPS tracker in her boot.

Standing alone with Knox, Dani flinched at every creaking board and dangling cobweb. She'd frozen in fear until the dog had rushed to her side. His presence infused her with courage.

Dani kissed Knox's head. "Thank you," she whispered.

Something was wrong. Walsh wouldn't wait this long. She dared not speak his name aloud, certain the kidnapper was listening in. Knox's powerful nose had brought him to her. But why was he alone?

A chill coursed through her with the sensation of someone watching her.

The kidnapper was here.

Her mouth went bone-dry.

Were there hidden cameras?

The house groaned as if it was tired of standing. Dani reconsidered her position on the steps and paused.

Tessa's desperate wails. She pivoted, searching for where the sound emitted, but the infant's cries echoed inside the cavernous space.

Were they coming from above or below? It was so hard to tell.

"Knox, let's find Tessa," she said, leaving the bags.

Dani gathered his leash, still dragging from his collar, and ascended the last step to the upper level.

The landing extended to the rooms on the opposite sides of the staircase, providing a balcony that looked down to the floor below. In the dim light, Dani struggled to see five feet in front of her. She used the burner phone to illuminate her path, testing the wooden boards before stepping on them.

They reached the first closed door, and she felt for the knob. It offered an ominous groan of protest, though Dani had expected nothing less. She inched it open and glanced inside. Sheet-covered furniture pushed against the wall added to the gothic ambience. Tessa's cries faded, almost muted, confirming the infant wasn't there.

The duo examined the upper floor until they'd exhausted the possibilities. They shifted direction, descending the stairs.

Tessa's wails were inconsistent. They started and stopped as though the kidnapper was trying to console her.

"Keep crying, sweetie," Dani whispered. She needed that audio to trace the baby's location.

With Knox at her side, Dani entered the main hallway. The kitchen stood to the right, and an ajar door to the left, revealing steps to the basement.

Tessa's howls intensified. Louder. More intense. Desperate.

"I'm coming, Tessa," she called.

Dani nudged the basement door open, and the rancid scent of mold and dirt wafted to her.

She aimed the phone flashlight at the concrete steps, but the fading glow wasn't helpful. Dani patted the wall, seeking a light switch, but found nothing.

Tessa's cries erupted from the depths below.

Encouraged, Dani and Knox descended.

They crossed the cement floor, Dani swiping at the cobwebs sticking to her face. "Tessa!"

When they reached the far side of the basement, she spotted a pull string and tugged. A single bulb came to life, illuminating the dank space.

A massive pallet stacked with boxes stood to her right. Dani withdrew her hand from the cord, dragging a sticky mess of spiderwebs at the same time. She flicked them away.

Tessa's cries stopped.

She shivered, scanning the dungeon-like room. "Tessa?"

Silence.

Knox panted beside her.

Again, the baby's ear-piercing wails erupted.

Dani hurried forward, bumping into crates and things.

Tessa's broken whimpers tore at her heart. "I'm coming. Dani's here."

She shoved past her fear, using her desperation to find Tessa, and continued the trek through the dungeon.

Dani pushed aside objects, searching deeper into the mess that threatened to tumble down around her. Mold and mildew assailed her senses. Dampness and adrenaline coursed through her body, making her tremble.

"Where is she?" Dani hollered.

She struggled to comprehend the infant's location amid the surrounding chaos. "Knox, seek!"

She'd never formally trained the K-9 in search and rescue. Asking him to find Tessa wasn't fair, but he was her last hope.

Knox obediently put his nose to the ground, sniffing a path to the opposite corner.

Dani ripped through boxes and trash. As she pulled at the remaining carton, exposing the cold cement floor, the source of the crying became clear. Not the sweet six-month-old infant in need of care, but a speaker wrapped in one of Tessa's blankets.

A lure designed to draw her there.

Dani stared in disbelief at the tiny box before lifting and inspecting the dark screen cover. As the child's incessant wailing continued, Dani's frustration erupted, and she flung the speaker with a scream.

The plastic shattered, silencing Tessa.

"No!" Dani dropped to the floor, Knox immediately at her side. "What have I done?" The only connection she had with the missing baby was gone.

Footsteps echoed above.

Was it Walsh? If she didn't call out, he'd never find her. "Walsh!" Dani hollered, bolting to her feet. She started for the steps. "I'm down here!"

The door above slammed shut.

Dani and Knox sprinted through the rubbish.

Yet the reality settled in before she reached the stairs.

The speaker was a lure to trap her in the basement.

The kidnapper wanted the weapons.

None of this made any sense.

Unless she was the intended target, and he planned to kill her.

Knox whined, always in tune with her emotions.

Rage and fear roiled through her, and Dani used the feelings to fight.

She lunged up the steps, tugging and pounding on the door. "Let us out!" Even as Dani said the words, she felt like a character in a B-rated horror movie. She slammed her hand against the wood, then kicked it for good measure.

Knox barked and growled his agreement.

Silence again.

The walls closed in around Dani.

"What do you want from me?"

Knox settled at her side with a whimper of understanding.

What was happening to them?

The single lightbulb flickered and died, thrusting Dani and Knox into inky darkness.

"God, help us." She reached for Knox, grasping his leash like a lifeline. "We have to find a way out."

They descended into the frigid basement. Dani lifted the cell phone in a last ditch effort at producing light. They stepped cautiously through the trash, seeking any means of escape.

Dani spotted a narrow rectangle of a window.

Hope ignited. Spiderwebs and dust covered the glass. In the days before egress window regulations, the small opening would've been normal. Today, it prevented her from escaping the dungeon. Dead flies peppered the web, testifying to the impossible task of leaving this place.

Dani shivered, forcing down her terror, and assessed the situation. Boxes and bins stacked beneath the sill would help her reach the window, but the minuscule size prohibited her getaway. Knox wouldn't fit through, either.

Dani looked for anything she could use to ram the door above. Junk filled the basement, but she found nothing helpful. Terror cloaked her and, if not for Knox's presence, Dani might've completely lost it.

"Breathe," she reminded herself. "Breathe." Dani pressed her hand over her racing heart. She had to calm down before she hyperventilated.

"Lord, help me!" The prayer was as heartfelt a supplication as she'd ever spoken. She squatted, wrapping her arms around Knox. The dog was all she had to ground her.

She wouldn't cave into fear and let this maniac win at his horrid game. Digging into her criminology training, Dani considered the man's motive.

Had he followed her into the house? He'd wanted to get her away from the vehicle and the task force. If the kidnapper had found the bags filled with Styrofoam and toy guns she'd left on the second floor, he'd locked her in the basement as punishment. She ripped the burner phone from her pocket and glanced down at it. No reception.

No way to call for help.

Panic rose in Dani, and she felt caught between screaming and having a complete breakdown.

"Lord, I can't fix this. I can't take any more!" she shouted at the rafters overhead.

The absurdity of it hit Dani with the force of a hurricane. Was that a threat to God? Would the Almighty throw up His hands and admit, Okay, okay, you win?

She froze. "That's how I treat You, isn't it? As though I'm the one in control, and You exist to answer my demands."

*Let God be Lord of your life.* The comment bounced to mind. It was part of the last Bible study Dani and Jayne had attended together. What did that mean? Weighed down by the circumstances and impossible task of escaping the basement, Dani sunk to the dirty cement floor.

She put her head in her hands. "Lord, people have hurt and disappointed me so many times that I've accepted pain as normal. I protected myself by being alone. Yet here I am. As brokenhearted as I was the day my dad walked out." Knox nudged her hand and Dani hugged him. "Lord, I surrender. I can't save myself. I need You to rescue me from this dungeon and in every way possible."

The plea encompassed her lost and broken dreams, and the ones she'd not allowed herself to hope for.

She swiped away a tear. "But more than that, Lord, I beg You to save Tessa and protect Walsh. I love them both. Please, my life for theirs, if that's what it takes."

Dani rested her head against her knees. An unexplainable peace soothed her aching heart. She loved Walsh. Always had. For the first time, confessing it brought relief.

Knox barked and raced over to the stairs. Dani jumped to her feet and followed.

Her reprieve immediately vanished at the acrid scent of smoke.

The house was on fire!

# SEVENTEEN

Walsh threw himself against the shed door with full force. After two more attempts, the wood splintered and gave way.

He flew through the shed's entry and landed with an oomph, knocking the wind from his lungs. With both wrists still bound behind his back, he couldn't brace for the fall.

Dani's screams reached him.

Walsh got to his feet in an awkward stumble. He inhaled the acrid scent of smoke before he spotted the red and orange flames stretching into the sky.

"Dani!" He bolted away from the outbuilding on wobbly and unstable legs, gaze fixed on the fully engulfed farmhouse. "Dani!"

Loud barking echoed and a black blur rounded the inferno, rushing straight for Walsh.

"Knox!"

Dani jogged with the dog, and Walsh wasted no time closing the distance between them.

"You're alive," he said, uncertain if he was hallucinating.

She smiled. "Here, let me help you." She moved behind him and, within a second, the bindings snapped free. "Learned that trick in hostage training."

Walsh pulled her into his arms. "Thank You, Lord." The heartfelt gratitude emitted easily from his lips.

"I can't find Tessa," Dani said, stepping back, head

hung. "He used a speaker to lure then trap me in the basement." She relayed the events leading to their reunion.

Walsh provided a recap of his own experience. "I hoped Knox would get to you before I passed out. How did you escape?"

They staggered away from the inferno.

"Knox." She smiled down at the dog. "He found a coal chute door disguised behind old furniture and we climbed out. He's brilliant." She stopped to hug the Dobie mix.

"But Tessa's gotta be near enough for the speaker to work, right?" Walsh asked.

"No, he probably used a recorder set on a loop or controlled it remotely with another device." Dani sighed. "It's hopeless."

"Negative, Chief. Nothing is impossible with God."

Knox emitted a low growl, gaining their attention. He stood rigid, staring at the copse of trees where Walsh had parked.

The group sprinted in that direction, and Walsh spotted a figure ducking into the shadows. "We'll never catch him before he escapes."

"We won't, but he will." Dani addressed the K-9, "Knox, hunt!"

The dog took off like a shot, leaving Walsh and Dani trying to catch up. The canine seemed to have ignited an internal turbo boost.

When they neared the man fleeing from Knox, Walsh called, "Stop! Police!"

The man ignored them, attempting to outrun Knox, who was quickly closing in.

He screamed as the Dobie mix launched into the air, tackling him to the ground.

Walsh and Dani finally reached the duo and found the guy flat on his face. Knox's teeth were clamped around his arm.

"Call him off!" the man shouted.

He wore a black long-sleeved shirt and pants, as well as a balaclava hood that covered his head. But something about his voice was familiar.

"Knox, release!" Dani demanded.

After several seconds and a few more tugs, Knox obeyed. He growled and took two steps back in a stalking stance.

Walsh approached and ripped off the hood, revealing the man's face. "Aiden DeLuca!" Walsh made no effort to hide his amazement.

Aiden cowered on the ground.

"Where is Tessa?" Dani towered over him.

Walsh feared she'd pummel the man. And he might let her.

Aiden raised his hands in surrender. "She's fine. She's fine!"

"Where. Is. She?" Dani stormed.

"She's safe in my car. Over by where Walsh parked," Aiden's voice quivered as he gestured a tentative finger in the direction of the tree line where a dark four-door sedan was partially concealed.

Dani sprinted for the car.

Walsh reached for Aiden. "Try that again, and we won't call Knox off when he gets you," he warned.

"Understood." Aiden nodded vehemently.

"Walk. Slowly." Walsh took his place behind Aiden and they followed Dani.

She ran to them, carrying Tessa.

Walsh exhaled. "Thank You, Lord," he uttered, and the prayer was imbued with more heartfelt gratitude than he'd ever spoken in his life.

"I didn't hurt her," Aiden whined.

"Do not speak," Walsh warned with the minuscule remnants of self-control he could muster.

Dani pinned Aiden with a look that could blast a hole through cement.

Aiden nodded, interpreting the meaning.

Walsh walked to his car and retrieved his cell phone. No service.

"Why doesn't my phone have reception?" he snapped at Aiden.

The man winced. "There's a device in my car that disrupts the signals. Just turn that off."

Dani sprinted to his vehicle and quickly returned with the small handheld gadget. She used the burner phone Aiden had given her to report the incident to 9-1-1 while Walsh notified the team using his cell.

"We've already sent backup," Eliana blurted. "Are you okay?"

"You're picking up my bad habit of skipping the greeting," Walsh teased.

"Sorry, we're worried over here!" Eliana said good-naturedly. "When Dani's tracker didn't move, we called for assistance."

Sirens wailed in the distance, confirming her words.

"We're fine and we have Tessa." Walsh launched into a speedy explanation of all that had happened.

"Outstanding!" Cheers from the team erupted over the line.

Walsh felt lighter than he had in days. "Will advise when we're en route."

"We'll be waiting at the condo," Riker promised. "We're so glad you're okay."

"God is faithful!" Tiandra called out.

Walsh laughed and disconnected before facing Aiden. He shook his head. "I really wanted to give you the benefit of the doubt."

"Why?" Aiden snorted. "Because we were once brothers?"

"Once a blue blood always a blue blood," Walsh contended.

"Right. Until the department retires you," Aiden muttered. "Then you fade to black, and nobody remembers you."

"Is that what happened to you?" Dani asked, joining them.

"Oh sure, at first coworkers, even old commanders, keep in touch. They bring you a few casseroles or desserts when you get home from the hospital." He grunted. "But then you're forgotten. As though you never existed. They go on with their lives, and you find out who your real friends are." Aiden averted his eyes. "And there aren't many."

Walsh's gaze flickered between Dani and Aiden.

Hadn't he been as guilty of forgetting those he worked with once they'd retired? And that's exactly what they would do to him when his day came too.

But he had time to deal with the upcoming change. Aiden's injury had forced him into the unwanted role without allowing him the time for an emotional transition. The department had thrown Aiden into the fire and abandoned him.

"I did my job, and it nearly cost me my life!" Aiden bellowed. "And for what? They handed me a check and took my career!"

"I'm truly sorry," Walsh said.

The softly spoken words seemed to stop Aiden in the middle of his rage. He blinked.

"I'm guilty of everything you said," Walsh replied.

"You didn't work with me," Aiden disputed.

"I'm at fault for doing those things. Got busy and forgot about you."

Aiden looked down. "My life was the badge I wore. When they stole that, I became a nobody."

"I sympathize with you, but it doesn't explain why you did this," Dani said. "Was it all you? Are there others working with you?"

Something flickered across Aiden's face.

"How do you plunge from being a decorated officer to a murderer?" Walsh asked.

"It wasn't supposed to go down like that," Aiden said.

"You tried to kill us both! Multiple times!" Walsh

boomed, suddenly angry again at the man's flippant attitude. "That's not a mistake or an accident."

"Figured Jayne confessed everything at the warehouse."

"You shot at us that night?" Dani clarified. "It wasn't Prachank?"

Aiden hesitated, as though trying to decide whether to work that angle. At Walsh's unwavering glare, he replied, "It was me. I meant to hit you, not Jayne."

Dani sucked in a breath and Walsh fisted his hands to keep from punching Aiden.

"I used Prachank's gun to throw you off the trail."

Walsh inhaled, digesting the information. "Wasn't Prachank involved?"

Aiden didn't respond, he continued rambling. "I couldn't find the missing munitions. You put Jayne in protective custody at the hospital. I reevaluated. I searched her place and found a few smaller pieces."

"Like the explosives you used at the cave?"

"I left the clues for the Decorah ice caves at Jayne's apartment and in her desk to lure you there. Away from your team." Aiden exhaled. "If you'd brought the firearms tonight, I never would've set the house on fire."

As if that was their fault?

"And when your bomb failed?" Walsh asked.

"I'll tell you who set the explosions at your headquarters," Aiden blurted as though Walsh hadn't spoken.

"What about the men who shot at us from the Kawasaki?" Walsh asked.

"What was Jayne's connection with you?" Dani said at the same time.

Aiden hesitated. "That's a lot more complicated. And they're not the only ones involved."

Dani inhaled, rubbing Tessa's back, and prayed before speaking. "You understand you're in deep here, Aiden. If you don't start talking, you will go down for all of it."

Knox shifted to her side, staring down Aiden. The man audibly swallowed. "I really cared for her. At first."

Dani bit her lip to keep from slapping him. He'd used Jayne.

"It's a long story."

"Then speak fast," Walsh growled.

"Jayne didn't have to steal the guns. Everything was working fine, until she ruined it," Aiden said. "I had to recover them. Thought she placed clues to where she'd hidden them."

Jayne's knowledge of Aiden's crimes, coerced or not, crushed Dani. All they had was his questionable word, unless she recovered.

Sirens grew closer, gaining Aiden's attention.

"Look, I'll talk. I know how this works. But I need a deal. I'll give up Prachank and the others involved, including my customers that I've sold weapons to," Aiden said. "But first, we deal. The criminals I've worked with will kill me in prison. Not to mention, I was a cop. That's like a double whammy!"

Dani didn't disagree.

"No way. We've got enough with you alone," Walsh said. "And if Jayne doesn't recover, we'll add murder to your charges."

"Wait!" Aiden pleaded. "There's a huge player. If you believe I pulled this all off on my own, you're giving me more credit than I deserve. Trust me, you want the big dog I work for."

At the word *dog*, Knox growled.

Aiden flinched.

"Speak first, then we'll consider bargaining," Dani said.

"Deal first or I'm not saying anything," Aiden challenged.

Police cruisers arrived on scene and the fire trucks pulled onto the farmhouse property.

"You're running out of time before I contact my lawyer," Aiden said, crossing his arms over his chest. "And once I do that, I'm not talking."

"Fine," Walsh said. "I'll request a deal with the DA if you offer the truth."

Aiden's gaze bounced between them.

"Be glad Walsh is a man of his word," Dani said. "I'd have thrown you to the criminals in jail and let them sort it out."

"Keep watch on him." Walsh said, "I'll be right back."

"He won't move, will you?" Dani replied.

"Nope."

Officers exited their vehicles, and Walsh hurried to talk to them, returning within seconds carrying handcuffs.

After reading Aiden his rights, he pulled the man to the side, cuffed him, then called the team. Eliana set things up to video-record the discussion, so they'd have Aiden's confession.

"Okay, go," Walsh ordered.

Aiden started. "I'm working with ATF commander Chuck Lewis. I assumed Jayne had told Chief Fontaine the truth, so I had to eliminate Chief Fontaine before she identified me. When you and Walsh came to my house, I realized you didn't know the details."

"So why the continued attempts?" Dani asked.

"Lewis ordered your deaths and set up the hits on your lives, including the HQ bombing. I didn't tell him the burner phone Jayne and I used to communicate with him was missing. It contained all the evidence of our conversations with Lewis. I figured Jayne hid it with Tessa. Except, I couldn't find it after I kidnapped her."

"That's why you were interested in Tessa's location and well-being?" Dani asked.

"Exactly." Aiden sighed. "The only way to get her stuff was to kidnap Tessa. But, honest, I didn't hurt her. I'd never harm a child."

Dani gaped at him. Was he serious?

"Tell me more about the burner," Walsh pressed.

"That phone will prove I'm telling the truth. Lewis provided us the details regarding which firearms to take and the buyers for each of them. He coordinated everything remotely from Washington, DC. He's got a lot of pull. Jayne and I were boots on the ground. Jayne had the connections with the other evidence

technicians, giving her access to the munitions."
Aiden shook his head. "Do you understand why I
need protective custody? Once you confront Lewis,
he'll have me killed. He abandoned Prachank to the
authorities! I'll be next."

"Is that why you dropped the phone number?" Dani
asked.

Aiden's confused expression conveyed the information was a surprise to him. "What?"

"You left it in the SUV when you broke into it at
Ledges."

Aiden cursed. "I'm such an idiot!"

"Is that all you need from him?" Dani asked.

"For now." Walsh led Aiden to the waiting officer.
"He's under arrest. I'll be right back."

Walsh returned to Dani and Tessa, still video con-
ferencing.

"This is far beyond anything we imagined," Tiandra said.

"Do you know Chuck Lewis?" Walsh asked Skyler.

"Not personally, but this isn't a shock. Rumors
about his corruption have bounced around inner cir-
cles for years," she replied. "And the number that you
found for the ATF headquarters would give Aiden
access to contact Lewis."

"We can't go breaking down doors and demand
Lewis confess," Chance arguably noted.

"Aiden's word won't hold much believability without that burner phone," Elijah said.

"He might just be trying to save himself." Graham
contended.

"True, Aiden's lied more than once," Tiandra added. "He's got every reason to weave a wild tale."

"But throwing Chuck Lewis under the bus?" Skyler asked. "That's a massive leap from inventing stories to cover himself."

"Lewis has the ability to orchestrate an operation like this," Riker said. "To take them down, we have to cut the head off this corruption beast."

"So, we look for the burner phone," Dani said.

"I'll accompany the officer transporting Aiden and ensure he's delivered to the marshals," Walsh said. "They'll keep him in protective custody. We'll meet you at the condo."

The team disconnected.

Walsh faced Dani, leaning in to kiss Tessa on the head. The move surprised Dani.

"I thought we were going to die in there," she confessed. "I really need to tell you something."

"Okay." He quirked a brow.

"All the things I once held dear disappeared, and it's hardened my heart." Dani paused, then continued. "Started when my dad abandoned us when I was a kid. You know that part."

Walsh nodded.

"When Aiden trapped me in that awful basement, I realized I've never trusted God to be in control of my life. I didn't want to get hurt again, so I protected myself right into loneliness. I released my fears to God and asked Him to take care of me."

"That's wonderful." Walsh's face softened. "I sort

of had an epiphany too. That can wait, this can't." He inhaled and said, "I'm in love with you."

Dani gaped, unsure how to respond. She'd longed to hear those words from Walsh. The courage to tell him that she also cared for him stuck in her throat. Terrified, she held her tongue. Once she spoke her feelings to him, there'd be no going back.

What if she wasn't good enough for him? Caring for Tessa was one thing. Loving a man like Beckham Walsh was another.

Marissa's explanation regarding Walsh's painful past left her hesitant. She couldn't bear the thought of breaking his heart.

After hearing Aiden's confession, Dani realized she'd misjudged Jayne. If she failed to see that deception in a friendship, how did she possess the skills to choose a healthy relationship?

Walsh might be the best person in the world, and he'd more than proved himself trustworthy. But Dani didn't trust her own judgment. If she was wrong, or he changed his mind about her, he'd destroy her heart.

She'd fallen hard for the man, decreasing her defenses and clouding her vision.

The hurt on his face warned that her silence had lasted a moment too long.

"We'd better get going," he said, disrupting the awkwardness. He turned on his heel, and she followed, feeling like she'd just made a huge mistake.

# EIGHTEEN

Sunshine poured through the condo's living room window. Dani cradled Tessa, gleefully consuming her morning bottle. Tiandra and Skyler had provided the overnight protection detail. The rest of the team had arrived before dawn, developing their plan. Only Walsh was absent due to a meeting with the marshal's office regarding Aiden DeLuca.

A mix of emotions washed over Dani. Grateful Walsh wasn't present and disappointed at the same time. She'd grown comfortable with him. Worse, she hated the way they'd left their relationship conversation in limbo.

*Get over it.* Once they completed this case and arrested Lewis, she and Walsh would return to their worlds, apart from each other. Wasn't that what she wanted? Yet, doubt lingered.

Dani sat Tessa upright and rubbed the infant's back to burp her.

The investigation had uncovered issues regarding the security and handling of evidence in her department's custody. And the first thing she'd rectify was a regular inventory with two-person accountability.

After Jayne recovered, her legal situation and whether she'd face a jail sentence remained an unknown. Dani planned to help with Tessa. Perhaps if Jayne had had that support earlier, she wouldn't have fallen prey to Aiden DeLuca's schemes. Regardless of what the man claimed, and Jayne's obvious mistakes, Dani wouldn't abandon her friend in her time of need.

Her new strategies ensured Dani wouldn't have the opportunity to bemoan the romance that couldn't happen between her and Walsh.

Riker paced a path between the kitchen and dining room. "Aiden's accusations against Lewis have our takedown on a timer."

Dani faced the group. "We must strike hard, fast, and without warning."

"Right," Chance agreed.

"How long will the marshals conceal Aiden's identity and location from Lewis?" Elijah asked.

"Only until we make our move," Skyler answered. "DeLuca's not officially under WITSEC protection." She reached for Tessa.

"Great." Dani passed the infant to her and stood. "Our timetable just accelerated."

"If Lewis learns about Aiden, his nefarious operation comes to a screeching halt," Graham noted. "We've got one shot at charging him. Any weak spots in the case and he'll escape conviction."

"Absolutely." Tiandra tapped the evidence board. "If only Jayne corroborated or refuted Aiden's claims, it would help."

"Jayne's involvement is undisputed. We just don't know to what degree," Dani replied, hating the way the words tasted like betrayal. "We need that burner phone."

Walsh entered, and Dani sucked in a breath. Her pulse quickened, and she averted her eyes.

"Morning. I brought breakfast burritos." Walsh held up the bag, wafting the delicious aroma to her and standing too close.

Dani plastered on a smile. "They smell wonderful."

"You're my hero." Eliana and Graham hurried to distribute the proffered food while Walsh perused the evidence board.

"Good work capturing the information we lost in the explosion." With his back to her, Dani surveyed Walsh's muscular frame and military-neat appearance. The group rallied around him, offering the minimal updates they'd discovered since the night before. Their respect for him impressed Dani. His handsome exterior matched his kind, thoughtful, and compassionate interior. The years hadn't diminished her attraction for him. As though sensing her perusal, Walsh glanced over his shoulder, making eye contact with Dani.

Skyler settled Tessa in her swing and moved to Walsh's side, discussing options.

Had Dani made a mistake ignoring his romantic interest?

Tessa's grunts gained her attention and offered an excuse to leave the room. Hoisting the infant, Dani carried her to the bedroom. She reminded herself that looking at Walsh in any context other than as a co-worker was unacceptable.

Yet, her emotions pleaded with her to reexamine her stance.

"Where is your paci?" Dani asked Tessa, spotting the pacifier connected by a clip on her car seat.

Dani retrieved it, detecting a lump in the seat fabric corner. Setting Tessa beside her, Dani removed the padded cushion, revealing a burner phone.

"Walsh!" She used Tessa's blanket to withdraw it.

He was immediately at her side. "What's wrong?"

"Check this out." Dani passed the device to him.

Walsh inspected the phone, careful not to contaminate the evidence. She leaned closer, smelling his cologne and pretending not to.

Her olfactory senses again had her second-guessing. Everything with Walsh felt right. Could they work through her insecurities together? She lifted Tessa who gripped a section of Dani's long hair and tugged. She chuckled, prying away the infant's steel hold, reminded that Tessa was her priority. With Jayne's condition and legal complications, a romantic distraction was out of the question. "Is it the device Aiden mentioned?"

Walsh frowned. "There are a series of numbers saved in the notes."

"Messages?"

"Only one." He held it up for her to see.

Dani sucked in a breath. "That's the original anonymous text I received at the start of this case!"

"Why would Jayne hide a cell phone with nothing on it?" Walsh asked, heading for the living room. He placed the device into a clear plastic bag, then each member examined it. "Dani found this hidden in Tessa's car seat."

"Is it the burner Aiden used to communicate with Lewis?" Elijah asked.

"There's no call history," Eliana said.

Graham quirked his brow. "What're the series of numbers saved in the notes section?"

"Evidence logs for other weapons?" Tiandra guessed.

Elijah shrugged. "Account numbers for money drops?"

Walsh added the suggestions onto the evidence board. "All good ideas—keep them coming." He paused and hurried to look at the phone again. "Wait." A slow grin spread over his lips.

The group stilled. The clock on the wall ticked away the seconds.

"You're killing us, Walsh," Dani urged.

He winked at her. The simple notion made Dani weak in the knees.

"Type in the first number as a GPS coordinate," Walsh instructed Eliana.

Eliana tapped rapidly on her keyboard. "Yes! Winterset, Iowa, is coming up." She continued searching. "The others aren't working."

"We've got a place to start," Walsh said.

"Is it the location of the missing munitions?" Excitement encompassed Graham's tone.

"Road trip!" Riker stuffed the rest of his burrito into his mouth. "Ready to work, Ammo?" The Dutch shepherd trotted to his side.

"Maybe the other numbers are a ruse?" Skyler asked.

"Riker and Chance, follow Dani and I," Walsh said. "We're not going in without backup."

"Hey." Skyler put her fists on her hips. "That's marshal discrimination," she teased.

"Sorry." Chance laughed, leashing Destiny.

"Take my SUV." Skyler passed Chance her keys.

"Skyler and Tiandra, you work the Fed angle." Walsh leashed Knox. "Uncover Lewis's activities, involvement, and travel schedule."

Dani glanced down at Tessa.

"Leave her with us." Tiandra reached for the baby. "We'll take good care of her."

Dani relinquished hold of the infant. Though she feared leaving her again after what had happened, she trusted God was in control.

The group loaded into two SUVs, driving east-bound on Interstate 80 toward Iowa.

Dani could barely contain her eagerness on the two-hour drive. Always in tune with her, Knox sat perched with his head poking through the divider. Dani stroked his velvety ears, easing her anxiety. When they entered the driveway for the neglected green clapboard house amid a copse of dead trees and ugly yellowed grass, she was practically crawling out of her skin.

"There?" Dani leaned forward.

Walsh parked at a distance from the structure and dialed Riker on speakerphone.

"Yeah, boss."

"Recon before we head in. We'll keep watch outside."

"Roger that." Riker pulled up behind him.

Thin boards braced the weathered awning over the

door. The connecting fields reflected abandonment. On the opposite side of the road, acres of soybeans and open pastures flourished.

The two marshals with their K-9s approached the house, returning a few minutes later.

"All clear."

Dani and Walsh holstered their guns and exited the SUV with Knox.

The wind kicked up around them, whistling through the trees. Dirt clouded the scene. "Where'd that come from?" Dani shielded her eyes with her hand.

Riker and Chance investigated the interior of the house. Dani and Knox took one side of the perimeter, Walsh the other, and they met on the backside. Knox strained against his leash, moved to the far end of the property, then backed up and dropped to a sphinx position.

"Walsh. Be still." Dani inched closer. "Knox, seek."

The dog rose and repeated the alert. They investigated, spotting blue barrels hidden within a grove of overgrown lilac bushes. "Good job, Knox!"

He wagged his back end enthusiastically.

"Bombs?" Walsh asked warily. "Riker and Chance!"

The men hurried up to them.

"Knox alerted," Dani said.

"Hold on! Skyler had us bring her SUV because she has something for just such an occasion." Chance ran toward the vehicle, returning with a crowbar and a little robotic gadget in hand. "ATF uses these to check for bombs," he explained, setting the device on the ground.

The group stepped backward while Chance piloted the robot with a remote control, circling the barrels. A series of long beeps preceded his announcement. "It's not a bomb."

Riker and Walsh used the crowbar to remove the tops of the barrels. "Bingo!" Walsh exclaimed.

Dani scurried closer, spotting the firearms that filled each drum. Chance and Riker documented the discovery while Dani removed the cell phone taped to the inside of the last barrel. "It's dead."

"Knox. Down." Dani gave him the accompanying hand command. Riker and Chance repeated the order for Ammo and Destiny. The dogs dropped to sit, panting softly and waiting for their next assignment.

"I've got a universal charger in the SUV," Walsh said.

They rushed to his vehicle and plugged in the device, bringing it to life. A litany of threatening texts and voicemails from Lewis to Jayne provided the evidence they needed.

"Aiden wanted us to find this, but I bet he didn't realize Jayne had saved this message," Dani said, pointing to Aiden's text dated several months prior.

Tell the authorities, and Tessa pays with her life.

Walsh's eyes narrowed. "He thought he'd put everything on Lewis and get away."

"We've got them!" Dani lunged into his arms,

whooping joyfully. They embraced for a few minutes, and she relished the moment. "I wasn't wrong about Jayne."

"No. You weren't." Walsh's breath was warm on her cheek, sending a shiver up her back.

Dani eased herself onto her feet, creating distance. "This proves they forced her participation."

A ringing interrupted them.

"It's the hospital." A lump lodged in her throat.

Walsh kept his arm on her shoulders as she answered, "Hello?"

"Chief Fontaine, this is Nancy. Jayne is awake and doing great!"

That afternoon, ATF commander Chuck Lewis looked down his pointed nose at Walsh, Dani, and Skyler. "You'd better have a stellar reason for storming into my office." Haughtiness rolled off the man in waves.

Walsh smiled. They had the evidence to apprehend him. This personal interview was icing on the arresting donut. "I'm sure you're aware that a significant quantity of stored munitions were reported missing from several Nebraska law enforcement agencies."

Lewis steepled his fingers. "Yes, such a disgrace to the chiefs responsible for those departments." He pinned Dani with a glower.

"Great news, though," she replied. "We've recovered them."

A flash of something akin to panic passed over Lewis's face. "Superb."

"Better yet, we traced all of it to a conspiracy within the ATF," Walsh said.

"That's why you're here?" Lewis's attempt at nonchalance flopped. "Write it in a report."

"You'll want to hear this in person," Skyler assured him.

"Jayne Bardot regained consciousness and is recovering," Dani said.

"Aiden DeLuca is in custody, and both will testify against you," Walsh added.

"That's preposterous!" Lewis's eye twitched.

Walsh passed the ATF commander a printed listed of the messages from the condemning phone.

"I have no idea what this is? What am I supposed to do with it?"

"Check out the texts and voicemails," Walsh replied.

The color drained from the man's pale face as he scrolled through the contents. Lewis audibly swallowed.

"We've already linked you to the crimes," Walsh replied. "Your only hope of any leniency is handing over Prachank."

"You're mistaken!" Lewis bellowed. "I'll have your badges for this vile accusation."

Skyler added, "Our technical expert obtained the electronic trail you left."

Lewis pushed away from his desk. "I see." Several silent seconds passed before he said, "I'll give you Prachank, but I want a deal."

"You'd be amazed how fast people talk when

they're trying to save themselves," Walsh said. "With or without your help, you're facing a lifetime behind bars."

"Where's Prachank?" Dani pressed.

Lewis exhaled, pausing as though considering his options. He scribbled on a piece of paper. "He's hiding at this address."

Walsh glanced at the information. Prachank was in Omaha, blocks from the decimated HFTF headquarters office. They'd been so close! He bit his lip from saying a word his mother would throttle him for and passed the document to Skyler. She offered a nod, then texted the team, already staging for the takedown.

"You and the AUSA," Walsh said, referring to the assistant United States attorney, "can work out your 'deal.' Although, he's seen the messages."

"Especially those to Jayne, threatening her innocent six-month-old baby if she failed to comply with your nefarious deeds." Dani crossed her arms. "You'll need to do some fast talking."

Lewis gawked and hung his head. At Walsh's signal, the arresting officers entered the room and took Lewis into custody.

Walsh had one more piece of unfinished business to handle.

An hour later, he and Dani stood at the airport gate, waiting for their flight.

"Are you going straight to the hospital when we arrive in Omaha?"

"Yes. Jayne's doing well, and I want to take Tessa

to visit her." Dani smiled. "Thank you again for the offer to help her find good legal representation."

"She got caught in something way bigger than her."

"With her confession, maybe the AG will have mercy regarding the charges," Dani said. "If not, Jayne is prepared to accept full responsibility for her involvement. She was relieved to admit everything about Aiden after living under his constant threats and intimidation."

"I'm still fuming that he lied and threatened Tessa's life if Jayne didn't comply with his orders," Walsh growled.

"Jayne was smart to compile and hide the evidence the whole time," Dani said. "When she realized Aiden had taken the illegal guns, she called me the night she was shot to confess and ask for help."

Walsh squeezed her shoulder. "Are you feeling better about taking on the role of guardian for Tessa?" He quickly added, "Just until she and Jayne are reunited?"

"Yes."

Walsh paused, working up the courage he needed. "I have to tell you something before we board our plane."

"Okay."

"I'm grateful for this case. God used it to teach me a lot about myself." He inhaled a fortifying breath. "I assumed my identity was in the badge I wore, or the title I held. And I was terrified to surrender them."

Dani nodded. "I understand."

"I realized who I really am isn't tied to those

things." He exhaled. "I guess that sounds dumb to you."

"Not at all. I'm glad you see the amazing man I've come to know you are." She offered him a side hug.

"Thank you."

"My turn." Dani's eyes shimmered. "You asked me a question I never answered."

Walsh blinked. He had more to say, but his throat went dry.

"I've always been in love with you, but the timing was never right. And after the Varmose investigation, I held my bitterness against you. That was wrong of me."

"No, it wasn't. I failed to be there for you and protect you from the aftermath." Walsh sighed. "I seem to have that MO."

"Come again?"

This was what he'd waited for. He had to let her off the hook. "I don't blame you for not wanting a relationship with a guy who's inept at caring for those in his charge."

"Marriage isn't about one person assuming complete responsibility for another's life and safety. It's about a partnership, helping each other."

Walsh stared at his boots. If only that were true.

Dani touched his arm, and he met her gaze. "You needed love and support too."

He swallowed hard.

"What happened with Gwen was tragic. Mental health issues are complicated. You did the best you could at the time. It wasn't your fault."

At the release, Walsh's chest constricted, and his eyes stung.

"How about if we both lay down our pasts and stop nursing old grudges?" Dani asked. "I think God's big enough to handle those and still give us a bright future. Together."

Had he heard her correctly? "I would love that."

"Remind me to thank Marissa," Dani said.

"For what?"

"She's wise."

Walsh chuckled, his emotions overflowing. "Yes, she is." He pulled Dani close, brushing her lips in an overdue and heart-awakening kiss.

The speaker overhead announced their boarding call, and they reluctantly parted.

Walsh glanced over Dani's head, spotting the group of strangers smiling at them. "I think we're a hit," he whispered.

Dani laughed. "We've waited too long for a lifetime together." She slipped her hand into his.

"Let's go home."

# EPILOGUE

*Two months later...*

HFTF assembled at the Walsh horse ranch with the blueprints for the renovated headquarters building spread out on the table.

"It's going to be better than ever." Eliana grinned.

"We'll have the option to add in necessary additions as the team grows," Walsh said.

"Enough talk about that," Marissa injected. "Celebration time!"

"Agreed. I'm drooling over that cake." Tiandra rolled up the prints while Elijah placed the massive dessert in the center of the table.

"Let's pray and dive into this!" Walsh said.

The team circled and lifted their voices in gratitude for closing the case, for Prachank's arrest and return to prison, and for Jayne's continued healing.

A knock instigated Knox's bark. "Thank you for the warning." Dani laughed, walking to the door.

Captain Bonn and Troopers Ulrich and Nguyen entered.

"Are we late?" Bonn asked.

"Nope, right on time." Skyler waved them in.

As Tiandra and Elijah passed hefty slices of the dark chocolate cake around, Dani said, "The one thing I can't shake is Aiden's claims that the law enforcement community abandoned him after his retirement."

"I need to make more of an effort to keep in contact with the retirees," Walsh said. "Especially since I'll be joining them soon."

"No way." Graham stabbed a hunk of cake. "You'll remain on staff as part of the newly developed HFTF board of directors."

Walsh chuckled. "We'll see." Dani inched closer to him. "You look like you're cooking up an idea."

"Two months of dating, and you already know me too well," she replied.

"I've had thirty years of studying you." He winked, and she leaned in for a kiss.

"Come on, you two, we want to hear the plan," Skyler probed.

They parted, and Dani grinned. "Actually, it's all Marissa's fault."

Marissa flopped onto the seat beside her. "Now that sounds negative. Reword it to say, 'It was Marissa's brilliant idea' instead."

"What? My soft-spoken, keep-to-herself, mind-her-own-business sister offered her opinion?" Walsh teased, earning him a swat from Marissa.

Dani chuckled. "Meadowlark Lane Ranch solidified a secret dream I've been praying about."

Marissa shot Walsh a wink. What did his sister know?

The group quieted, listening.

"Retirement is around the corner for me…" Dani began. Knox strolled to her side and dropped into his sphinx pose at her feet. "Ever feel like your dog can read your mind?" She laughed.

"All the time," Riker and Chance chorused.

"Bosco's aware of what I'll say before I say it," Tiandra joked.

"Exactly. They're amazing," Dani said. "Which brings me to my plan. I'm retiring from GIPD. I'll train comfort dogs like Knox to bridge the gap between retired and injured law enforcement personnel. It would provide them a connection to their blue brothers and sisters. The canines would offer mental and emotional support toward healing."

"I love that idea!" Skyler jumped to her feet.

"We'll help train them as handlers and assist with the canines too," Tiandra added.

"You'd do that?" Dani asked, eyes wide in surprise.

"I want in on this team," Ulrich quipped.

"Get in line," Bonn replied with a grin.

"Of course," Eliana said. "It's what family does."

Dani wiped at the moisture on her face. "You all are amazing."

"Since we expect to hear wedding bells soon, it's a natural progression," Marissa said.

Walsh's cheeks burned with heat.

"What?" Dani whipped around.

"Thanks, sis," Walsh growled playfully.

Marissa shrugged. "Sorry, I'm terrible at keeping great secrets."

"Excuse me." Walsh exited the room and collected the ring he'd bought for Dani.

He returned, feeling the weight of the team's stares.

Clearing his throat, Walsh approached Dani. He'd not intended to do this publicly, but his heart, and his sister, nudged him forward. "It's taken me thirty years to reconnect with the love of my life."

Dani gaped.

"Dani, if you'll take me, I'll spend the rest of our days loving you to the best of my ability."

She swallowed, eyes shimmering with tears.

Had he scared her?

"Give her the ring," Marissa whisper-yelled.

Walsh shot her a good-natured glare and opened the box. "Dani, will you marry me?"

Dani nodded then blurted, "Yes!" She flung her arms around his neck.

The group hollered their approval and the K-9s barked and bounced.

Walsh beamed at the joy of second chances and the incredible gift of family.

Then he captured Dani's promise with a kiss.

\* \* \* \* \*

*If you enjoyed this story,*
*be sure to check out*
*Sharee Stover's previous release,*

Seeking Justice.

*Available now from Love Inspired Suspense!*
*Discover more at LoveInspired.com.*

Dear Reader,

I hope you've enjoyed the Heartland Fugitive Task Force as much as I have. I can't lie, the dogs are always my favorite characters, and for this story, I wanted to focus on a different breed. My friend's Dobie mix, Duke, became the inspiration for K-9 Knox.

On a personal note, this book comes on the heels of a long season of transitions and change for our family. Change is hard! The retirement shift can be especially difficult for professionals and their families who have dedicated their lives to their careers. Perhaps that's why it's essential for us to keep our identities rooted in who we are in Jesus Christ because He is the same yesterday, today, and forever (Hebrews 13:8). We're safe with him regardless of our ever-changing circumstances. That's good news, friend!

I love hearing from readers! Please join my newsletter where you'll be the first to hear about my new releases and get behind-the-scenes features for my books. You can contact me and sign up at www.shareestover.com.

Blessings to you,
*Sharee*